THE MATH KIDS: AN UNUSUAL PATTERN

THE MATH KIDS:
AN UNUSUAL PATTERN
DAVID COLE

COMMON DEER PRESS
WWW.COMMONDEERPRESS.COM

Published by Common Deer Press Incorporated.

Text Copyright © 2019 David Cole
Illustration Copyright © 2019 Shannon O'Toole

Published in 2019 by Common Deer Press
3203-1 Scott St.
Toronto, ON
M5V 1A1

This book is a work of fiction. Names, characters,
places, and incidents are either the product of the
author's imagination or are used fictitiously.

Library of Congress Cataloging-in-Publication Data
Cole, David.-First edition.
The Math Kids: An Unusual Pattern / David Cole
ISBN: 978-1-988761-37-4 (print)
ISBN: 978-1-988761-38-1 (e-book)

Cover Image: © Shannon O'Toole
Book Design: Ellie Sipila
Printed in Canada

WWW.COMMONDEERPRESS.COM

FOR ALL MY EQUATIONS AND MATH CAMP
KIDS WHO HAVE LEARNED THAT MATH CAN
BE FUN (REALLY!)

CHAPTER 1

The first thing I noticed was how quiet it was. I expected there to be a bustle of activity and plenty of noise, but it was so quiet I could hear the squeaking of my right sneaker as we walked down the freshly waxed hallway. I could see Justin looking around, taking in everything we passed. There were framed photographs on every wall with grainy black-and-white images of famous criminals who had been brought to justice by the FBI: Bonnie and Clyde, Al Capone, Machine Gun Kelly, John Dillinger, and lots of others whose names I didn't recognize. We passed doors labeled Cybercrime, Tax Fraud, Terrorism, and Kidnapping. We went by a large cafeteria where agents were sitting at tables, finishing breakfast before starting their day. Even here, the volume was low as agents stared down at their cell phones or spoke quietly to each other over coffee.

Agent Carlson, who was leading the small parade of me and my friends, finally stopped at the end of the long hallway in front of a door marked Cold Cases. He opened the door and herded us through the doorway.

"Well, here we are," he said.

I looked around the room. Four large tables were covered with stacks of yellowing papers. The walls

were covered with old wanted posters with names I didn't recognize. A row of printers was overflowing with printouts. And one wall was lined with gray metal file cabinets with neat lettering across each drawer. Two men in matching gray suits looked up from their laptop computers as we entered.

Agent Carlson made the introductions.

"Kids, these are Special Agents Perkins and Wilson." There was a nod from each agent as their name was mentioned. "And these are the Math Kids: Jordan Waters, Stephanie Lewis, Catherine Duchesne, and Justin Grant."

The agents gave us a thorough look, like they were memorizing our faces for future reference.

Agent Perkins asked, "Duchesne? Wasn't that the kidnapping case you worked on recently?"

"Good catch, Dan," Agent Carlson responded. "It was Catherine's dad who was kidnapped."

"You made pretty quick work of that case, if I recall," Perkins said.

Agent Carlson smiled. "I got credit for the arrest, but actually it was the Math Kids who did all of the work. Mr. Duchesne sent a coded message that the kids were able to solve with their math skills."

"Impressive." Agent Perkins nodded, looking at us with newfound respect. "So, what brings you to Cold Cases?"

"Care to explain, Jordan?" Agent Carlson looked my way.

How was I supposed to know? I'm just a fourth-grade student at McNair Elementary School. All I really knew was that Agent Carlson had asked us if we wanted to work for the FBI, although I guess "volunteering" is more accurate since, as Justin had correctly pointed out, we weren't getting paid.

"Agent Carlson thought we might be able to help with an old case that has some math in it."

"Wait, you're not talking about the Robbins bank robbery case, are you?" Agent Wilson asked.

"That's the one," Agent Carlson said with a smile.

"Good luck with that." Agent Wilson shook his head. "We haven't been able to make any progress on it at all."

I saw Justin's eyes light up. We had started the Math Kids club because we all loved math and solving problems.

"I don't know if we'll be able to solve it, but we'd love to try," I said.

"Great, then let's let these guys get back to work and we'll get started," said Agent Carlson.

We settled in at one of the long tables. Justin pulled out notepads and pens from his backpack so we could take notes.

Agent Carlson proceeded to outline the case that had baffled him and the other FBI agents working in Cold Cases.

"Fifteen years ago, there was a bank robbery in Dallas, Texas. Two men wearing masks and carrying shotguns entered the bank just as it opened on a Saturday morning. They pushed the customers and bank tellers into the manager's office. While one of the robbers kept an eye on their captives, the other forced the bank manager to open the vault and load up large duffel bags with cash."

Justin interrupted with a question. "How much did they steal?"

"It was a little over two million dollars," the agent replied.

Our mouths dropped open. None of us could comprehend that much money, especially in cash.

"They were preparing to make a clean getaway," the agent continued, "when the bank's security guard walked into the bank carrying a drink holder with four large cups of coffee. The guard saw the men and went for his gun, but one of the robbers clubbed him over the head with a shotgun and the two made their escape."

"Did they leave any clues behind?" Stephanie asked.

"Not a trace. They wore masks, so no one could give a good description of the two men, and they wore gloves, so they didn't leave any fingerprints. Despite the best efforts of the police and the FBI, no trace was ever found."

"But how we can we help?" asked Stephanie. "We're just kids. We don't know how to catch a bank robber."

"It's not about what happened at the bank that day, Stephanie," Agent Carlson said with a smile. "It's what happened twelve years later."

"Twelve years later?" she asked.

"Three years ago, one of the bank robbers died."

"How do you know it was one of the bank robbers?"

"Simple. He told us," the agent explained. "Walter Robbins had a change of heart as he was dying in his hospital room. He wanted to make up for the bank robbery, even though he insisted until the end that he was not the one who knocked out the security guard. He confessed his crimes to the FBI before he died."

"What about the money? Did you get it back?" I asked.

"No. When he found out he was dying, he left all his savings to the Dallas Veterans Hospital."

"Well, at least the money went to a good cause," Justin said.

"Since the robber died, the case is closed, then, right?" I asked.

"Except for the other robber," said Agent Carlson. "And the other million dollars."

"Did Robbins say who the other robber was?" asked Catherine.

"Or where the money was?" added Stephanie.

"No, but I think he was trying to tell us," the agent answered.

"Trying to tell us? What does that mean?" I asked.

"He left us a poem," Agent Carlson said, adding, "and that's where the Math Kids might be able to help."

The agent pulled a single sheet of paper out of a thin file folder labeled First National Bank of Dallas. He placed it on the table and we all crowded around to read it.

I've lived a life with many faults; I've tried to fix a few
My partner in the theft of vaults? I'll leave you with a clue
It's hidden in the middle of a dessert that's not sandy
No pattern there, and GPS won't come at all in handy
More difficult to find than a single grain of sand
Slipping through your fingers, the digits on both hands
To make a shape you need at least these to arrange
Add it makes it bigger, but multiply doesn't change
The wonders of the ancient world so many miles away
The colors soar above us on a sunny rainy day
Up or down it stays the same, but on its side, it goes and goes
The only prime that stands alone as everybody knows
Now it's time to start, right where the clues do end
Is anybody smart enough to call upon my friend?

There was silence in the room while we read and reread the poem. Agent Carlson finally broke the silence.

"So, Math Kids, any ideas?"

We looked at each other but nobody said a word. We had agreed to volunteer for two reasons. First, we were hoping to get some cool FBI stuff. Justin really wanted a badge. I was pretty sure that was out of the question, but maybe we could at least score some FBI jackets or hats. The second reason was that Agent Carlson had gone to bat for us with the classroom bullies and we owed him one.

Those reasons didn't matter now, though. All I could think was that we were in way over our heads on this one.

CHAPTER 2

We met in the school library after school the next day. For three hours, we stared at the poem Agent Carlson had given us. Three hours of reading and rereading the words, trying to figure out where to start. Three hours and we had come up with absolutely nothing.

"I think the bank robber was just having a little fun with the FBI," Justin complained. "There's nothing in the poem that makes any sense."

I was about to agree when I heard the library door open. I glanced at the clock and saw it was almost six o'clock. I waited to hear Old Mike call out to us in his loud, jovial voice. Old Mike was the janitor at McNair Elementary. He wasn't that old, really, but he had been at the school as long as anyone could remember. He got his nickname because people were always saying things like "Old Mike will take care of that" or "see if Old Mike can find it." Old Mike was always there in the morning when we got to school and was usually the last one to leave at the end of the day, and I don't think I've ever seen him when he wasn't in a great mood.

Instead of our friendly janitor, though, I was surprised to hear a raspy growl instead. "What are you kids still doing in here?" a man's voice barked out. "School was over three hours ago."

We looked up at the bearded man standing over the table. He had a frown on his face and smelled like he had just stepped out of one of the trash dumpsters behind the school.

"Well?" he asked gruffly.

"We were just leaving," I stammered. "I guess we didn't realize how late it was."

"What grade are you in?"

"Fourth."

"And you still don't know how to tell time?" He sneered. "Go on, now. Get out of here."

We scooped up our papers from the table, grabbed our backpacks, and left the library as quickly as we could. The man watched us from the hallway until the exit door had closed behind us.

"Who was that?" I asked as soon as we were safely on our way home.

"I don't know, but it sure wasn't Old Mike," Justin answered.

"Maybe he was sick today," Catherine said.

"No, I saw him this morning when I took the attendance slip down to the office," Stephanie added. "He was in the principal's office."

"Well, I sure hope he's back tomorrow," Catherine said.

But Mike wasn't in the next day. We saw the bearded man as soon as we entered the school. He was wiping down the glass display cases just inside the front door. He stopped what he was doing and stared at us as we stepped through the doorway. Old Mike would have called out a jolly "good morning" to us, but the bearded man just stared as we hurried past him to our classroom.

"There's only one way to find out what's up with Old Mike," Justin said.

I nodded in agreement. We had to ask Susie McDonald.

Susie's mom was the president of the PTO and always knew everything that was going on. Some people said that it was Mrs. McDonald, and not the principal, who really ran the school. The teachers and staff were afraid of her because she knew all the school board members and didn't hesitate to go to them if things didn't go her way.

"He was fired," Susie told us when we asked.

"Fired? But why?" I asked in surprise.

"He was stealing from the lockers," Susie said loudly, loving all the attention for knowing something the rest of the class didn't.

"What is there to steal? Pencils and paper?" I challenged.

"My mom said he stole one hundred and fifty dollars from a fifth grader's locker," Susie said, bringing oohs and ahhs from the crowd starting to gather around her. "Phil Duke brought it in to pay for his spring field trip to space camp."

"Why do they think it was Old Mike?" Catherine asked.

"My mom said he also stole a backpack from Tyler Stevens and a cell phone from Jackie O'Keefe," Susie continued, ignoring Catherine's question.

There were murmurs from the whole class as everyone gathered around Susie to hear more. Susie dropped her voice to a whisper so that everyone had to lean in even closer. "My mom said he may even go to jail."

"But why do they think it was Old Mike?" Catherine persisted.

"My mom said that he's the only one with a master key to all of the lockers," Susie said.

"But that doesn't prove he did it," I protested.

"And they found the backpack and cell phone in Old Mike's closet!" Susie said in a dramatic voice. "Can you believe it? Stealing from students?"

"No, I can't believe it!" I responded loudly. "Old Mike would never do something like that."

"But my mom said…" Susie began.

"Yeah, well your mom says too much if you ask me!" Justin said sharply, cutting Susie off in midsentence.

Everyone in the class gasped and then looked at Justin. They were probably all thinking the same thing, but Justin had been the only one brave enough to say it out loud. Susie turned a bright shade of red and was about to respond when Mrs. Gouche walked into the classroom and told us to take our seats.

I don't remember anything Mrs. Gouche taught us that morning. All I could think about was poor Old Mike. I just couldn't believe he would steal from students. But how could we prove it so Old Mike could get his job back?

At lunchtime, the Math Kids sat at one of the tables in the back of the cafeteria. We didn't want to be disturbed while we discussed the situation, and what, if anything, we could do about it. Justin suggested a petition that all the students and teachers could sign, but Stephanie didn't think that would work if the school board thought he was guilty.

"The evidence is definitely stacked up against him," I said, "but I still can't believe he would do something like that."

We were downhearted as we thought about it. Old Mike always had our backs when it came to the bullies. He had a knack for showing up whenever we were in trouble. Maybe it was all coincidental, but I had a feeling he was watching out for us.

"I just wish there was some way we could help him," Catherine said.

"The only way to help him is to prove that someone else did it," Stephanie argued.

"Or maybe there's another way to look at it," Justin said thoughtfully. "We don't need to prove that someone else did it. We only need to prove that Old Mike *didn't* do it."

"But isn't that the same thing?" Catherine asked.

"Not if there wasn't a crime to begin with," Justin said.

Stephanie, Catherine, and I looked at each other—the same puzzled expression on each of our faces.

The bell rang before we could ask Justin what he meant. I caught up with him on the edge of the playground. He was walking slowly, with one hand brushing the fence, and he responded with "um hmm" when I brought up our lunch discussion. I have known Justin long enough to know that he was in the "zone." Sometimes he became so deep in thought that he would tune everything else out. I also knew it was useless to try to talk to him when he was in the zone, so I went back over to where Stephanie and Catherine were talking.

"He's in the zone, isn't he?" asked Stephanie, looking over at Justin walking along the fence.

"Yep."

"What do you think he meant?" she asked.

"You've got me," I answered. "We've got money, a backpack, and a cell phone stolen from lockers. Why wouldn't he think those are crimes?"

We continued to discuss Justin's perplexing statement while we watched him from a distance. He followed the fence all the way to the end of the soccer fields, then made a left, and finally another left to walk back toward the school.

"Why do you think he does that?" Catherine asked.

"You mean walking along the fence?" I asked. "It's so he doesn't get lost."

"No, seriously," Catherine responded.

"I am being serious," I said. "In second grade, before they put the fence up, Justin started walking that direction and just kept walking. He told me later that he was trying to figure out what to do for his science fair project. Anyway, he just kept thinking and walking and thinking and walking and ended up almost a mile away from the school. He looked up and he was in a neighborhood he didn't recognize and had no idea how to get back."

"Are you kidding?" laughed Stephanie.

"Nope—totally serious," I said with a grin. "Luckily, Jimmy Woodside's mom noticed Justin sitting on the curb and brought him back to school. When I asked Justin what had happened, all he said was that his science fair project was going to be on how the shape of an ice cube affects how quickly it melts."

WHAT DO THINK ABOUT JUSTIN'S SCIENCE FAIR PROJECT IDEA? HOW DO YOU THINK THE SHAPE OF AN ICE CUBE WOULD AFFECT HOW QUICKLY IT MELTS? SEE THE APPENDIX TO LEARN HOW TO DO YOUR OWN EXPERIMENT.

CHAPTER 3

On Saturday, we had an emergency meeting of the Math Kids. We were planning to meet anyway, to continue working on the case of the bank robber's poem, but now we had something more important to do. We had to find a way to help Old Mike. It was our first chance to talk to Justin about his strange statement at lunch the day before.

"What did you mean when you said maybe there wasn't a crime in the first place?" Stephanie asked.

"Oh, I think there was a crime," Justin replied. "I just think the crime might not be what everyone wants us to believe."

"Well, that clears things up," I said sarcastically. Now I was more confused than ever.

"Hear me out for a minute," Justin said. He grabbed a marker and went to the whiteboard. "Here's what we know."

He wrote his thoughts down on the whiteboard.

FACTS

1. Phil said someone stole $150 from his locker
2. Tyler's backpack was found in Old Mike's closet
3. Jackie's cell phone was found in Old Mike's closet

"So, what's the crime?" Justin asked.

"That's easy," I said. "Someone stole stuff from kids' lockers."

"What if someone didn't really steal the backpack and cell phone?" Justin asked. "What if they were just put in Old Mike's closet to distract everyone from the real crime?"

"You mean stealing the hundred and fifty dollars?" Catherine asked.

"I don't think anyone stole any money," Justin said quietly.

"But you wrote it down as a fact on the board," Stephanie protested.

"No, I wrote 'Phil *said* someone stole a hundred and fifty dollars,'" Justin said.

Everyone went silent as what Justin was saying sunk in. The backpack and cell phone were found in Old Mike's closet. Those facts were hard to dispute. But we only had Phil's word that money was stolen from his locker. The money hadn't been found in the closet with the phone and backpack.

"Are you saying that Phil made up a story about the money being stolen?" Stephanie asked.

"And then took the backpack and cell phone and put them in Old Mike's closet so everyone would believe his story," I added. "But why don't you believe Phil?"

"LeBron James," Justin said.

Catherine and Stephanie just stared at Justin, baffled. But I was beginning to catch on. Justin is one of the shortest kids in the school. Even some of the first graders are as tall as he is. But Justin is a huge basketball fan. It is his favorite sport, even though he knows he will never be tall enough to play. His favorite player in all of basketball is LeBron James, and there is nothing he wants more than a pair of LeBron James shoes. There are only two things standing in his way. First, his feet are too small for even the smallest size of LeBron James shoes. And the second reason? The shoes cost about $150.

"Did you happen to see Phil's shoes today?" Justin asked with a smile. "Looked like a brand-new pair of LeBron James sneakers to me."

"You think Phil spent his space camp money on shoes and then made up a story about the money being stolen so his parents wouldn't be mad?"

"That's exactly what I think," Justin said.

"But that means Phil must have known how to get into their lockers," I said.

"How do you think he figured it out?" Stephanie asked.

"The same way we're going to," Justin replied. "We're a math club, aren't we? We'll use math."

Justin's plan was simple, but brilliant. If the locker combinations were completely random, there would be 64,000 possible combinations ($40 \times 40 \times 40$) since the three numbers could be anything from 0 to 39. But, since the codes were changed every year, he thought there was probably a pattern to how they were programmed. We knew four combinations between us, so maybe we could figure out the pattern based on that. Stephanie wrote the numbers on the board:

Stephanie	20 – 12 – 7
Jordan	10 – 25 – 13
Justin	10 – 36 – 16
Catherine	10 – 9 – 12

We were immediately excited by what we saw. Three of the combinations started with the number 10. If the codes were random, there was almost no chance that three of them would start with the same number. That meant there was probably some pattern used to set the number sequence. But why was Stephanie's different?

"I'm new!" she shouted as she figured it out. "I wasn't here at the start of the year, so my locker isn't in alphabetical order like everyone else's. It's not even in the same hallway as yours."

"That's it!" Catherine chimed in. "Our three lockers are in hallway A, and our combinations all start with ten. Stephanie's locker is in hallway B and her combination starts with twenty.!"

"That makes sense," I agreed. "Phil, Jackie, and Tyler are all in hallway C, so I bet their combinations all start with thirty."

We were on to something, but that only took care of one number out of three in each combination. Was there a pattern to the other two numbers, too?

We tried out a lot of ideas over the next few hours, but we couldn't come up with a pattern for the other numbers. We did come up with a plan, though. We were going to watch carefully as the kids around us opened their lockers. If we could add a few more combinations to our set of data, we might get the information we needed to find the pattern.

For the next few days, we hung around the lockers as much as we could. But even though we watched kids open their lockers, we were unable to see the numbers they were entering without looking suspicious.

Old Mike's replacement continued to stalk around the halls throughout the day. It seemed that every time we turned around, he was staring at us with his beady eyes. While Old Mike had made sure the side entrances to the building were open thirty minutes before school started, the new janitor only opened the main doors, forcing us to go around to the front of the building each morning. Old Mike had let us stay in the library for hours after school, but the new guy checked every room after school and made sure everyone was out of the building within thirty minutes of the last bell ringing.

"We've got to find a way to prove Old Mike didn't do it," Stephanie said as we left the school that afternoon. "I can't take much more of this guy. He gives me the creeps."

We were all in agreement, but how could we figure out the pattern for the last two numbers in the combinations?

CHAPTER 4

We had run into a brick wall with the locker combinations, so we decided to focus on the bank robber poem at our next Math Kids meeting. It was Catherine's idea to put the locker problem aside for now.

"Sometimes when I get stuck on a hard problem, I put it away and work on something else for a while," she explained. "Often when I come back to it, the solution is sitting right there in front of me."

We also decided it might be easier to make sense of the poem if we broke it down into smaller parts.

"The first two lines look pretty straightforward," I said as we read from the poem

I've lived a life with many faults; I've tried to fix a few
My partner in the theft of vaults? I'll leave you with a clue

"He feels bad about what he's done in his life and

is trying to fix it. He is clearly trying to give us a clue about how to find his partner."

Everyone agreed with that assessment of the puzzle, so we moved on to the next two lines.

It's hidden in the middle of a dessert that's not sandy
No pattern there, and GPS won't come at all in handy

This proved to be a lot harder. While the first two lines were clear, the next two were much more mysterious.

"Anybody have any ideas on this?" I asked.

"Well, we know the clue is hidden in a desert," Justin offered.

"That part is easy," Stephanie replied. "It's the second part of that line that doesn't make any sense. What kind of desert isn't sandy?"

"Antarctica," Catherine said, drawing puzzled looks from all of us. She went on to explain: "I know it sounds weird, but Antarctica gets less than eight inches of precipitation each year, making it the driest desert in the world."

"You don't think he's hiding in Antarctica, do you?" Stephanie challenged.

"Maybe. The next line says that GPS won't come in handy, so that would make sense, wouldn't it?"

We decided to set those two lines aside for the time being and moved on to the next two lines.

More difficult to find than a single grain of sand
Slipping through your fingers, the digits on both hands

"Great," Stephanie said sarcastically. "First there's no sand and now we have to find one grain of sand. That's like trying to find a needle in a haystack."

"Worse than a needle in a haystack," Justin said. "Given enough time and patience, you could eventually find a needle."

"You could use a magnet," I suggested, drawing a look from Justin.

"My point is," he continued, "that trying to find a grain of sand is impossible. That's why I'm not sure this guy really wants us to find his partner in crime."

"Well, we have to assume he does. Otherwise there's no point in continuing, is there?" Catherine said.

There were nods all around, so we went on.

"What about the second part of the line?" I said. "That's worded kind of strange, isn't it? What do you think he meant by 'the digits on both hands'?"

"It's the number ten!" Catherine said excitedly. "I mean, what else could he be talking about? There are ten fingers on two hands."

We all nodded in agreement, but solving one part of the puzzle just raised more questions. Ten what? Was the number ten a part of some equation? Not wanting to get bogged down, we moved on to the last eight lines.

To make a shape you need at least these to arrange
Add it makes it bigger, but multiply doesn't change
The wonders of the ancient world so many miles away
The colors soar above us on a sunny rainy day
Up or down it stays the same, but on its side, it goes
and goes

The only prime that stands alone as everybody knows
Now it's time to start, right where the clues do end
Is anybody smart enough to call upon my friend?

"It looks like there are six more clues here," Justin said as we finished reading the poem. "I think I know what one of them means, but not the other ones."

We all looked at him expectantly, but Justin continued to look down at the poem.

"Well, what clue did you figure out?" I finally asked.

"The only prime that stands alone," he said. "I think it's the number two because that's the only even prime number. All the rest are odd."

That's the second clue with a number for an answer," I pointed out.

"Maybe all the clues point to numbers," Stephanie said thoughtfully. "And the numbers are..."

"The way to find the other robber!" Catherine finished excitedly.

An internet search yielded the answer to the clue about the wonders of the ancient world. These were "must see" attractions from thousands of years ago, and we lost track of time for a while as we learned more about them.

There were seven wonders of the ancient world: the Great Pyramid of Giza, the Hanging Gardens of Babylon, the Statue of Zeus at Olympia, the Temple of Artemis at Ephesus, the Mausoleum at Halicarnassus, the Colossus of Rhodes, and the Lighthouse of Alexandria. Of the seven, only the Great Pyramid still stands, and scientists and archeologists still don't have

a definitive answer on how something so massive was built with such precision more than 4,500 years ago.

DO YOU WANT TO LEARN MORE ABOUT THE SEVEN WONDERS OF THE ANCIENT WORLD? CHECK OUT THE APPENDIX AT THE END OF THE BOOK.

Stephanie came up with an answer to "the colors on a sunny rainy day."

"The colors in a rainbow," she said. "There are seven of them. Roy G. Biv."

"Who's this Roy Biv guy?" Catherine asked.

"Roy G. Biv. It's a shortcut to remember the colors in a rainbow. Red orange, yellow, green, blue, indigo, violet. Roy G. Biv."

"We're on a roll," I said with excitement.

"If our answers are right," Justin said, bringing me back down to Earth.

"They're pretty reasonable answers, though," Stephanie responded. "It makes sense that these are number clues, especially if we have to solve some kind of equation."

"But the poem doesn't give us an equation to solve," Justin argued.

"We'll worry about that later," Catherine said. "In the meantime, anyone have any clue about this shape clue?"

We worked on that clue with no results until Justin's mom called down to ask if anyone wanted lunch. Justin's mom was a great cook and we were starving, so we were happy to adjourn for the day. Over our lunch of sloppy joes, applesauce, carrot sticks, and cold glasses of milk, we switched our thoughts to how we could help to clear Old Mike's name. We agreed to continue working on the pattern of the locker numbers over the rest of the weekend.

"Look at the bright side," Justin said with a smile. "With only two numbers to figure out, there are only sixteen-hundred combinations."

"Maybe we just need a little luck," I said.

As it turned out, luck was exactly what we got.

CHAPTER 5

On Monday morning, Stephanie was five minutes late getting into the classroom. Mrs. Gouche was busy getting things set up to start the day, so she didn't notice Stephanie slipping into the room.

As Stephanie passed my desk, she said, "I think we found that luck we were looking for."

I was left wondering for the rest of the morning. We didn't have our math group that morning, so it was lunchtime before I could ask her what she meant.

"I was trying to open my locker this morning and couldn't get the combination to work," she said excitedly. "I tried it three times before I realized I was at the wrong locker."

"So?" Catherine asked.

"I knew I was at the wrong locker by looking at the locker number."

"But how is that lucky?" I asked.

"Well, we know the first number depends on the

hallway. What if the other numbers have something to do with the locker number?" she asked.

"That would allow them to use some kind of formula to create the combinations!"

"Exactly!"

"What do you think, Justin?" I asked.

The smile that came over Justin's face gave me my answer. He thought we were onto something.

After school, we stayed late in our classroom to add the new data we had. We knew we didn't have much time before the mean new janitor made his rounds, so we worked as quickly as we could. We started by writing all the information on the board. We found that being able to see the information made it much easier to see patterns.

	Combination	Locker Number
Stephanie	20 – 12 – 7	412
Jordan	10 – 25 – 13	265
Justin	10 – 36 – 16	196
Catherine	10 – 9 – 12	129

"Wait, I think I might have something for the third number in the sequence!" Justin yelled suddenly, startling all of us. "You just have to add them up."

"Add what up?" I asked, but Catherine got it before Justin could answer.

"Add up the numbers in the locker number." She grinned.

I looked carefully at the locker numbers and then I saw it, too. If I added up the digits in Stephanie's locker number, I got the third number in her combination. We checked, and all the other lockers conformed to the same formula.

Stephanie	$4 + 1 + 2 = 7$
Jordan	$2 + 6 + 5 = 13$
Justin	$1 + 9 + 6 = 16$
Catherine	$1 + 2 + 9 = 12$

Two numbers down and one to go. We were ready to tackle the final number in the combination when we heard a loud crash in the hallway!

We rushed to the door and saw the new janitor sprawled on the floor in a puddle of soapy water. He was holding his knee and looked to be in a lot of pain.

"Are you okay?" Catherine asked.

The janitor's face turned an angry shade of red. He painfully rose to his feet, using the mop handle to steady himself. He scowled at Stephanie and limped a few steps toward us before stopping.

"How many times I gotta tell you kids to get out of the school? What's wrong with you? The bell rings, you go home—can't you get that?"

We didn't wait to hear any more. We were already out the door and heading down the hallway. Behind us, we could hear him muttering angrily to himself: "What kind of stupid kids don't go home when school is over?"

We were out of the building and halfway across the playground before any of us realized we had left our backpacks in the classroom.

"Not only that," Justin added, "but we also left our locker combinations written on the board. That means anybody, including that creepy janitor, can get into our lockers."

"So, what are we going to do about it?" I asked.

"We're going back in to get them," Stephanie said defiantly.

I looked at her in amazement. Stephanie is one of the bravest people I have ever met. Even though I have only known her for a couple of months, I've seen her stand up to the bullies, our teacher, an FBI agent, and even a kidnapper!

"If she's going in, then so am I," Catherine stated firmly.

Justin and I looked at each other and shrugged. We were a team, so it looked like we were all going back in. But how were we going to sneak in without being caught?

We walked back to the side door by the playground and pressed against the wall to stay out of sight. Justin knelt and peeked through the glass door.

"Coast is clear," he said. "If we're quick, we should be able to get to our classroom, grab our backpacks, and erase the board before he sees us."

The plan was simple enough. It just depended on speed, a little luck...

...and the door to be unlocked. Which it wasn't.

"Okay, on to plan B," I said.

"What's plan B?" Justin asked.

"You got me. I just know plan A didn't work," I said with a grin.

Justin laughed, but quickly grew serious again. "If he's already locked the side doors, that means we're going to have to go in the front."

"And that's a big problem because that means we'll have to go down the main hallway and he'll easily be able to see us," I said.

"We need a diversion," Catherine said.

"What are you thinking?" Stephanie asked.

"We need to get the janitor to one end of the building and away from the main door," Catherine answered. "Then someone can sneak in, erase the board, and grab the backpacks."

"But how are they going to get out without being caught?"

"Simple," Justin said. "The side door to the playground opens from the inside."

"One question: who's going to go in?" Stephanie asked.

Justin and I looked at each other, nodded, and said "spoof" at the exact same time.

"What is spoof?" Stephanie asked.

"It's a game," I answered. "It's sometimes called three coins."

I explained the rules. Each person hides zero to three coins in their hands and extends their fists. Then everyone guesses the total number of coins held by all the players. Each guess must be different than previous guesses. If someone has already guessed five, for example, no one else can guess five. Whoever guesses the right number is out. The game continues until only one person remains. The last person standing loses the game.

I could tell that Catherine and Stephanie were a little skeptical.

"We've never played before," Stephanie said. "How do we know there's not some trick to winning all the time?"

"It's a fair game," I promised. "It's just simple math with a little luck thrown in."

"Okay, we're in," Catherine said. "Loser grabs the backpacks, right?"

We all agreed. Since we didn't have coins, we used pebbles we found on the playground.

"Is there an advantage to going first?" Stephanie asked.

"Not really," I answered, "except that if you get the total right no one else can guess that number, so I guess that could be an advantage. We switch who goes first each round, though, so that keeps it fair."

Justin went first, guessing eight. Stephanie guessed seven, and Catherine guessed nine. Since I wasn't holding any pebbles in my hand, I decided to go for a lower number and chose six. We opened our hands to reveal seven total pebbles. Stephanie was out.

In the second round, Catherine guessed first with

five. Since I didn't have any pebbles again, I guessed lower with four. Justin went with six. He and Catherine were both holding three pebbles, so Justin's guess was correct, and he was out.

That left just Catherine and me. I tried to figure out her strategy. She had held three pebbles both times so far. Would she change and maybe go with something else this time? And what should I do? I had held zero both times. Would she expect me to go with something else?

It was my turn to guess first. I guessed three. This was the safest guess because it didn't give away anything about how many pebbles I was holding. If I had said four, for example, she would know I was holding at least one pebble. If I had said zero, she would know I was holding no pebbles. Catherine looked at my face closely, trying to see if I would give anything away about how many pebbles I was holding.

"Two," she said, opening her hand to show two pebbles. I opened my fist to show an empty hand. I was the one going in.

CHAPTER 6

As it turned out, the plan would take all of us. First, we needed to get the janitor away from the front door so I could sneak into the school without being detected. After that, it would all be up to me.

I hid by the front door. Stephanie stood at one corner of the school. From her position, she could see Catherine at the rear of the building. It was Stephanie's job to signal me when the coast was clear. It was Catherine's job to signal Stephanie from the back of the building. That left Justin to create the diversion. He needed to get the janitor to the back of the building.

He knocked loudly on one of the back windows. Nothing.

He pounded on the back door. Nothing.

In frustration, Justin picked up a fist-sized rock. He looked down at it, considering the consequences of what he was about to do. Before he had time to think about it any longer, he threw the heavy rock through the back window, resulting in a loud crash that could be heard throughout the school.

Justin took off as fast as his short legs could carry him, just making it around the corner of the building when the back door flew open and the janitor burst out into the sunlight, his face a picture of rage.

Catherine, who had ducked around the corner of the building as the janitor emerged, frantically waved her arm at Stephanie, who in turn signaled me. I had heard the crash, but didn't know the cause, so I was terrified to enter the building. I knew my friends would risk everything for me, though, so I had to come through for them. I pushed the front door open and stepped inside. Trying to keep as quiet as I could, I eased the front door shut behind me.

The janitor was nowhere in sight, but I could hear yelling from the end of the hallway. I ran as fast as I could toward our classroom, hoping that he wouldn't hear my pounding feet. I had just rounded the corner that took me from the main corridor to the hallway where our classroom was, when I heard loud footsteps coming my way. He must have heard me! Our classroom was at the end of the hall, but I didn't think I could make it there in time. *What should I do?*

I ducked into the first door I saw, only realizing once I got inside that it was the girls' bathroom. I could hear the heavy stomping of boots. It had to be the janitor! I quickly stepped into one of the stalls and quietly pulled the door shut behind me. I heard the door to the bathroom slam open and bang against the wall.

"Who's in here?" the janitor yelled. "Show yourself!"

I only had seconds before he would find me. I quietly stepped up onto the toilet seat so he wouldn't see me if he looked under the door of the stall. I was too terrified to think about how disgusting it would be if my foot slipped and plunged into the toilet bowl.

I could hear him getting closer. It was only a matter of time. He was between me and the exit, so there was no way out. Now I could see his shadow through the crack in the stall door. In a moment he would push the door open and that would be it for me.

"Hey!" someone yelled from the bathroom doorway. "What do you think you're doing in the girls' bathroom?"

I couldn't see who it was, but it sounded like Stephanie. The boots turned toward the door and I could hear sneakered footsteps retreating down the hall. The janitor took off in hot pursuit. I waited until the bathroom door closed behind him before I made my move. I hopped down from my uncomfortable perch, pulled the stall door open, and, after a cautious look around, crept quietly to the door of the washroom. Peering out, I saw the coast was clear. I sprinted down the hall and pushed open the door to our classroom.

I quickly erased the board and grabbed the four backpacks, grunting a little under the weight of Justin's loaded pack. He did insist on lugging around everything but the kitchen sink!

I listened carefully but didn't hear any sound in the hallway. It was now or never. I stepped quickly into the hall and made a run for the back door. I pushed the release bar and I was out. Stephanie was waiting for me. She grabbed two of the backpacks and we ran across the playground toward the gate in the fence. Only when I closed the fence behind us did I feel safe. But where were Justin and Catherine?

I was considering going back to see if they needed help when I heard a loud whisper from a clump of shrubbery near the fence.

"Over here!" Justin's voice came from the bushes.

Stephanie and I ducked behind to join him.

"Where's Catherine?" I asked.

"Right behind you," came Catherine's voice from behind a thick tree trunk.

"Can we get out of here now?" I asked.

"You don't have to ask me twice," Justin said.

CHAPTER 7

The next day at school, Justin and I noticed the back window was now boarded up with a thick piece of wood. The blood drained from Justin's face as we walked past. I could tell he was thinking about how much trouble he would be in if anyone found out he was the one who broke the window.

"Don't worry, buddy, your secret is safe with me," I reassured him.

"What secret?" he asked. Justin put on a look of total innocence, causing us both to break out in laughter.

I was still chuckling as I followed Justin through the front door of the school. I almost ran into him as he abruptly stopped.

"What's going..." I started, but then saw why he had stopped. The new janitor was standing just inside the door with Principal Arnold by his side.

"Those are the kids," he said, pointing a meaty finger in our direction.

"Justin and Jordan, can I see you in my office?" Mrs. Arnold asked.

We followed her past the school secretary's desk and into her office. Mrs. Arnold motioned toward the two chairs sitting in front of her desk. We sat down and waited for her to lower the boom on us. She looked at both of us for a long moment before speaking.

"Is there anything you'd like to share with me?" she asked.

This was the oldest adult trick in the book. They ask a question then just back off and wait for a confession. Overall, Justin and I were pretty good kids, but we'd been in enough trouble in our lives to know that the only defense was to act like we had no idea what they were talking about.

I looked over at Justin and he had put his look of total innocence back on. I almost laughed but managed to keep a straight face.

"I'm not sure what you mean, ma'am," Justin said.

"Me neither," I added.

"Did you notice that the back window was boarded up?" she asked.

"Yes, ma'am," I answered. I had also learned that it was best to keep my responses short and sweet in times like this. The more you said, the more likely you were going to say something that was going to get you in trouble.

She gave us another long look, her gaze moving back and forth between us.

"Mr. Swenson tells me you two were here late after school yesterday afternoon," she said.

"Who is Mr. Swenson?" I interrupted before she could continue.

"He's the new janitor," she responded.

"What happened to Old Mike?" Justin asked, trying to divert the principal into a different conversation.

"That's not important right now," she said.

"It's important to us," I said. "Old Mike didn't do anything, and we can prove it!"

"You can?" she asked in surprise.

Justin looked at me like I had gone nuts. He knew we couldn't prove anything right now.

"Well, maybe not yet, but we know he didn't do it," I said defiantly.

"So, were the two of you here late after school yesterday?" Mrs. Arnold asked.

"Yes, ma'am," Justin answered. "We were working on a math problem." Which was completely true.

"But we left the building when the new janitor yelled at us," I added. Which was also true, although I conveniently left out the part about us returning to the building.

"And you weren't responsible for a rock being thrown through the window?" she asked, fixing her stare directly on me.

"No, ma'am," I answered truthfully, hoping she wasn't going to ask Justin the same question.

She didn't, though, and I breathed a quiet sigh of relief because I'm not sure if Justin would have been able to lie in response to a direct question from the principal.

"And I guess you didn't see anyone throw the rock, either?" she asked Justin.

"No, ma'am," he answered firmly. "I didn't see anyone throw a rock through a window."

I had to bite my lip to keep from smiling. Justin hadn't seen anyone throw the rock because he had thrown it himself. We'd both answered her questions truthfully. It wasn't our fault she had asked the right question to the wrong person.

Mrs. Arnold looked at us without saying anything for a long time, hoping we would break the silence. Justin and I kept quiet, though, and she finally gave up trying to get us to say anything incriminating.

"Okay, then, you'd better get to class," she said.

"Yes, ma'am," I responded quickly, and, just as quickly, we were out of her office. Neither of us said anything until we were around the corner and halfway down the hallway to our classroom.

"That was close," Justin said.

"Too close," I agreed.

"Do you think Mr. Swenson saw us?"

"I don't think so. We were the last kids at the school, so he just assumed it was us."

"Pretty good assumption in this case," Justin said with a smile.

We walked on in silence, deep in thought. We needed to get the janitor problem solved soon because the next time we might not be so lucky.

Unfortunately, the Math Kids were not able to meet over the weekend. Spring break had started and my parents were dragging me to my Aunt Jeanette's house for four long days. Normally, that would be fine because I get along with my cousins just fine, but it meant I wouldn't be able to make any headway on the two problems hanging over our heads.

Justin was also booked up. His parents were taking him to Washington, DC. While he always enjoyed touring the Smithsonian, especially the National Air and Space Museum, it wouldn't leave him with any free time to spend tracking down the remaining bank robber or finding a way to clear Old Mike's name.

"With both of us gone over the break, it looks like it will be up to Stephanie and Catherine to keep things on track," I said.

"I think we're in good hands with those two," Justin replied.

CHAPTER 8

As we later discovered, Stephanie and Catherine had things well in hand—at least when it came to the locker combination problem.

"Well, with Justin and Jordan out of town, I guess that means it's up to us to make some progress," Stephanie told Catherine as they settled onto the couch in Catherine's living room.

"What do you want to tackle, the poem or the locker combinations?" Catherine asked.

"Let's go with the locker combinations," Stephanie answered, adding, "I think we're really close to a solution on that one. We've got two of the three numbers figured out."

Stephanie wrote out what we knew on a sheet of paper.

	Combination	Locker Number
Stephanie	20 – 12 – 7	412
Jordan	10 – 25 – 13	265
Justin	10 – 36 – 16	196
Catherine	10 – 9 – 12	129

First number is hallway (10 for A, 20 for B, 30 for C)
Second number is ???
Third number is sum of digits in locker number

The two girls stared at the information, trying to uncover the secret of the second number in the combination. The grandfather clock in the corner was the only sound as it quietly ticked off the minutes. There were several moments of excitement as one of them thought they may have solved it, only to find out the pattern didn't work with all the combinations.

Adding the last two locker numbers and multiplying by the first worked for Stephanie's combination, but not for the others.

Squaring the last locker number worked for Jordan and Justin's combinations, but not for the girls.

Using the first and third digits of the locker number worked for Jordan's combination, but not for anyone else.

"Maybe there isn't a pattern after all," Stephanie finally said in frustration, after almost an hour of trying different formulas to come up with a solution.

Catherine disagreed. "There has to be a pattern, or else how was Phil able to get into the other lockers?"

"What if he found a way to get the list of combinations from Old Mike?" Stephanie argued. "For all we know, he might have the list taped up on the wall in his closet."

"I don't think so," Catherine said. "We found patterns for the first and last numbers of the combination, so why not the second number?"

"Wait a minute," Stephanie said excitedly. "If the first and last numbers are right, look how much we've narrowed down the possibilities. We started with sixty-four thousand combinations and now we're down to forty!"

Catherine didn't respond. Something that Stephanie said had triggered some connection in her brain. She stared at the locker numbers and combinations on the sheet, then off into the distance. Then back to the numbers, and off into space again. Stephanie started to say something about her friend going off into the "zone" like Justin, but stopped when she saw a huge smile come over Catherine's face.

"Nice work, Stephanie," she said.

"Me? What did I do?" Stephanie replied in confusion.

"You said the number forty," Catherine said, still grinning.

"What? What's so magical about the number forty?"

"It's just the secret to how to get the second number," Catherine said. "What happens when you divide your locker number by forty?"

Stephanie grabbed a pencil and quickly did the long division. "You get 10.3, but how..."

Catherine interrupted her. "I don't want the decimal value," she said. "All I'm interested in is the remainder."

Stephanie looked at her solution and quickly saw what Catherine had already seen.

"The remainder is twelve!" she yelled.

"And the second number of your combination is..."

"Twelve!" she shouted again.

They worked through all the locker combinations and the pattern worked for all of them. The second number was just the remainder when the locker number was divided by forty.

Catherine and Stephanie high-fived.

"This calls for a celebration," Stephanie said. "Too bad the guys aren't here so we could show them what you found."

Catherine sat contentedly back on the couch. A small smile played across her lips.

"Thanks, Stephanie," she said quietly.

"Don't thank me. You figured it out," Stephanie replied.

"I don't mean that," Catherine said. "I mean thanks for convincing me that girls can be good at math."

"Oh, I think you already knew that. You just needed a little reminder."

"Well, thanks for the reminder then," she said, then added with a big smile, "What would you say to a piece of chocolate cake and milk?"

"I'd say yes, of course."

Over thick slices of cake and tall glasses of cold milk, they discussed the next steps. Now that they knew how to get into any locker in the school, how could they use that information to help Old Mike clear his name and get his job back?

CHAPTER 9

The Math Kids met in Justin's basement the Saturday following fall break. It was great to hear that Catherine had cracked the code for the final number in the locker combination, but we still needed to come up with a plan for getting Old Mike his job back.

"Why don't we just go to the principal and tell her we know that Phil Duke is responsible," Catherine suggested.

"But what's our proof?" I asked. "We can't just say that we figured out how to open any locker in the school."

"Why not?" she countered.

"Because that doesn't prove that Old Mike didn't do it. The stuff was found in his closet, after all."

"That's a good point, Jordan," Stephanie said. "We need a way to get Phil to confess."

"What if we tell him?" I asked.

"Better yet, why don't we *Tell-Tale Heart* him?" Justin said thoughtfully.

Stephanie and Catherine looked puzzled, but I thought I saw where Justin was going with this. He and I had read a scary story by Edgar Allan Poe called *The Tell-Tale Heart*. In the story, the narrator had killed an old man and buried him under the floor in his house. When the police came to investigate, they didn't find anything. But as he sat with the police, the narrator thought that he could still hear the old man's heart beating—so loudly, in fact, that he was sure the police could hear it, too. So he lifted the floor boards to show the police where he had buried his victim. In the end, it was his own guilty conscience that made him confess to the crime.

"You think we can get him to hear Old Mike's beating heart?" I asked with a smile.

"That's the plan," Justin said with an evil grin.

Since we knew how to get into any locker in the school, our plan was to leave messages inside Phil's locker to scare him into confessing. We spent the next hour carefully laying out what the messages would say.

We knew it had to be Catherine or Stephanie who put the notes in the locker because Mr. Swenson was keeping a good eye on Justin and me. We decided to use that to our advantage. On Monday morning, Justin and I arrived at school early and announced our presence with loud talking as soon as we entered the building. Mr. Swenson heard us and immediately came to the front of the building to make sure we weren't up to any mischief. Knowing he couldn't follow both of us, we split up. The janitor followed Justin to the library and stood in the doorway while my friend browsed through the shelves. He wasn't looking for anything, but we knew the janitor would stay to keep a careful watch on him.

While Justin was in the library and I was keeping watch at one end of hallway C, Catherine and Stephanie were prepared to enter locker 619. We had followed Phil the previous week and knew it was his locker.

Catherine carefully entered the combination into the keypad. First, she entered 30 for hallway C, then 19 (the remainder when she divided 619 by 40), then 16 (the sum of the digits in the locker number). She pushed up on the handle of the locker and it opened!

"Whew, this thing stinks!" Catherine said as she pulled the door open. "Why don't boys ever take their gym clothes home to wash?"

"Just put the note in there before anyone comes," Stephanie said in a loud whisper.

Catherine placed the note on the center shelf of the locker where she was sure it wouldn't be missed.

The note read:

Are those new shoes worth the price Old Mike paid?

Catherine quietly closed the door with a click, and then, using the sleeve of her sweatshirt, she wiped the keypad and the locker handle.

"What are you doing?" asked Stephanie.

"Wiping off my fingerprints," Catherine answered. "You can't be too careful, you know."

Stephanie giggled as she and Catherine headed back toward the main hallway.

The first note had been planted. The question was how Phil would react when he saw it.

CHAPTER 10

With nothing to do but wait to see Phil's reaction to the note we had placed in his locker, we turned our attention back to the mysterious poem left by the dying bank robber. We met at Catherine's house after school.

"Hey, dad, is it okay if the Math Kids use your office for our meeting?" she asked.

Mr. Duchesne chuckled. "Well, it's not like I owe you kids anything. All you did was rescue me from two kidnappers."

We laughed as we entered his office, but our laughter quickly turned into oohs and aahs as we looked at the large wall of bookshelves, all crammed full of math books.

"Wow, look at all these!" I said as I skimmed through the titles. There were books on linear algebra, number theory, topology, non-Euclidean geometry, numerical analysis, set theory, probability and statistics, artificial intelligence and machine learning, and other topics I couldn't even pronounce.

"My dad has read every single one, and even wrote six of them himself," Catherine said proudly. "His specialties are number theory and machine learning, but he says it is important to be well-rounded in other mathematical areas, too."

"There are at least a dozen books devoted to pi," Justin said in amazement. *"A History of Pi, The Joy of Pi, Pi-Unleashed,* and even a French book called *Le Fascinant Nombre Pi*—unbelievable."

"Yeah, my dad is just a little obsessed with pi."

"Well, it is a pretty important number," Justin said. "People have used it for thousands of years to calculate the circumference and area of a circle."

"True, but there's much more to pi than just circles," Catherine said earnestly. "My dad told me that pi is related to the formation of all kinds of patterns, like the shape of rivers, the stripes on a zebra, and the spots on a leopard."

"That's really cool," exclaimed Stephanie.

"One of my dad's favorite pi stories is about a French man named Buffon and his loaf of bread."

"Bread? What does bread have to do with pi?" I asked.

"Well, as Buffon was walking home from the store with his groceries, a loaf of French bread fell out of his bag and rolled across a line on the sidewalk. Most people would have probably just thrown the bread away. But Buffon was a mathematician, so instead he picked it up and threw it back over his head onto the sidewalk. He did this for hours, writing down the number of times the bread landed on a line and the number of times it didn't. He used this data to come up with a formula that allowed him to estimate pi."

> ## DO YOU WANT TO RUN YOUR OWN EXPER-IMENT TO ESTIMATE PI? SEE THE APPENDIX TO LEARN MORE.

"Ah, I see you're telling your friends about Buffon's needle," Mr. Duchesne said as he entered the office. "It's one of my favorite math stories—and I have a lot."

"You can say that again," said Catherine.

"It's one of my favorite math stories—and I have a lot," Mr. Duchesne repeated with a wink.

We groaned good naturedly at his lame joke.

"People must have thought Buffon was a little crazy," I said.

"I think all mathematicians are a little crazy," Mr. Duchesne replied. "Our job is to find patterns where no one else can see them. That's a little crazy, right?"

"That sounds like this bank robber poem—you know, the one I told you about," Catherine replied. "We're trying to see how the numbers we're finding in the poem fit together into some kind of pattern."

"Except the poem says there is no pattern," Justin said.

"That would be pretty unusual," Mr. Duchesne said thoughtfully.

"Why do you say that?" Stephanie asked.

Catherine's dad went on to explain: "Because there are patterns all around us, Stephanie. Patterns in nature

that are described by the Fibonacci sequence. Artists and architects naturally found the most beautiful shape as described by the golden ratio without ever knowing the mathematics behind it. In any given list of numbers, no matter what they are, if you look long enough, you will see a pattern emerge."

"Always?" Justin asked.

"Almost always, anyway," Mr. Duchesne answered. "Here's an example: take any group of related numbers. I don't care if it is stock prices, city populations, lengths of rivers, heights of buildings, or anything else you can group together. No matter what the numbers are, you'll find that about three out of ten of them will start with the number one. Numbers starting with two are the next most frequent. Then three, and so on."

"But if they are random numbers, shouldn't there be a one out of nine chance of any number from one to nine being the first number?" Justin countered.

"It makes sense, right? But in fact, the numbers are six times as likely to start with one than to start with nine. This doesn't make sense if the numbers are random," Mr. Duchesne explained, adding, "but maybe they aren't truly random. Maybe hidden under the surface is a pattern we just haven't seen yet."

"Do you think the bank robber was lying when he said there was no pattern?" Justin asked.

"Maybe. Or maybe he doesn't know how unusual it would be to not have a pattern," Mr. Duchesne said as he started to leave. He stopped just inside the doorway and said, "Unless…"

"Unless what?" Justin prompted.

"Unless we're talking about numbers like my old friend pi."

With that cryptic end to the conversation, Mr. Duchesne was out of the door.

"Do you know what your dad was talking about, Catherine?" Stephanie asked.

Catherine explained that pi was a number that went on forever without any pattern to the digits.

"I guess that makes sense," I said. "The poem says there's no pattern. But I don't see how pi has anything to do with it."

"Maybe it would help if we wrote down what we know so far," Justin said.

We used Mr. Duchesne's whiteboard. Stephanie wrote, since she had the best handwriting.

Bank robber's poem
Clue is hidden in the middle of a dessert with no sand?
There's no pattern and GPS won't help?
Impossible to find clue? (finding single grain of sand)
10 - digits on two hands
? - to make a shape you need at least these to arrange
? - add makes it bigger, multiply doesn't change
7 - number of ancient wonders
7 - colors in the rainbow
? - up or down stays the same, but on its side goes and goes
2 - the only prime that stands alone

We were pretty sure that the clues all pointed to numbers, but three of them still had us stumped.

I was focused on the clue about addition and multiplication.

"What number makes it bigger when you add it, but not when you multiply it?" I asked.

This time it was Stephanie who figured it out.

"It's easy," she said. "The number one!"

Of course! When you add one to a number, it gets bigger, but when you multiply a number by one, it stays the same. Stephanie had nailed it! That left only two clues to solve.

"To make a shape," Catherine said, "you need sides. Like a square has four sides, a pentagon has five, and so on."

"That makes sense," Justin agreed. "But the clue

says you need 'at least these.' I don't get what that even means."

"Three!" shouted Catherine, drawing a look of surprise from the rest of the Math Kids.

"To make a shape with sides, you have to have at least three of them. You can't make a shape with just one or two sides."

That made sense. A triangle was the shape with the least number of sides.

"What about a circle?" Justin countered. "A circle only has one side, just curved around."

"True," Stephanie said, "but then you're really not arranging the sides, are you?"

Catherine agreed. "Good point, Stephanie. Also, the clue says 'at least these,' which would mean more than one, wouldn't it?"

"Only one more to go," I said, but before I could go on, Justin chimed in.

"Correction. No more to go," he said.

We all looked at him in anticipation. Had he figured out the last clue?

Up or down it stays the same, but on its side, it goes and goes

"What number looks the same right-side up or upside-down?" he asked. We all shouted a different number.

"Zero."

"One."

"Eight."

"Everyone is right so far," Justin said. "Now, how do those numbers look when you lay them on their side?"

This one stumped us for a bit. A zero laid on its side still looked kind of like a zero, just a little squashed. A one looked like just a straight line going sideways. But the eight—that was a different story. An eight laid on its side looked like ∞.

"That's the symbol for infinity!" I yelled.

"Right," grinned Justin. "And infinity doesn't end, right? You might say that it 'goes and goes.'"

High fives all around. We had the last number! The problem was, we didn't know what to do with the numbers now that we had found them.

We all looked at the clues, trying to find anything that would help us spot a pattern. If there even was a pattern, that is.

Justin, who is one of those people that can spot even the smallest detail out of place, noticed something wrong in Stephanie's notes.

"You spelled *desert* wrong," he said. "It only has one *s*."

I certainly hadn't noticed that, but then my spelling skills were nothing to brag about. Math came easy to me, but English and spelling weren't my strong subjects. Stephanie was about to use her finger to erase one of the *s*'s but stopped just before she did it. She looked at the poem carefully, then back at the board.

"I didn't spell it wrong. The bank robber did."

We looked at the poem and saw Stephanie was right. The bank robber had spelled it with two *s*'s, not one.

"It's a common mistake between *desert* and *dessert*," Justin said. "I only remember which one is which because of a trick my mom taught me. *Dessert* has two *s*'s because dessert is something I want more of. So it's the one with the extra *s*."

"What if it's not a mistake?" I asked.

"It must be. If it were a dessert, you wouldn't have to say it wasn't sandy," Justin replied.

"What if that was just to throw us off track?" I asked. "I mean, look how much care he took in coming up with this puzzle. I don't think he made a mistake. I think he spelled it just the way he wanted to."

"But that doesn't make any sense," Justin argued. "How can you hide a clue in a dessert?"

I read two lines of the poem out loud.

It's hidden in the middle of a dessert that's not sandy
No pattern there, and GPS won't come at all in handy

"I don't think we're looking for a location," I said. "It tells us that a GPS won't help us, so it must not be a place. I think we've been focusing on the wrong part of these lines."

"What should we be looking at, then?" Stephanie asked.

"Simple," I said, as a broad smile came across my face. "We're looking for a dessert with no pattern."

"A dessert with no pattern?" she asked.

"Exactly. And Catherine's dad has already given us the answer—pi."

It all made sense. In our third-grade class, we had celebrated March 14 as Pi Day, since it was the third month and fourteenth day, and the digits of pi start with 3.14. As part of Pi Day, our teacher had brought in miniature pies for us to eat as a treat. And, like Catherine's dad had mentioned, pi didn't have a pattern. Its digits went on forever without repeating.

"It fits with the next two lines, too," Justin said excitedly. He read them out loud.

More difficult to find than a single grain of sand

Slipping through your fingers, the digits on both hands

"I get it!" Stephanie yelled. "Since pi goes on forever, finding a clue in the numbers would be more difficult than finding a grain of sand in a desert."

"Great," Justin said sarcastically. "So how are we supposed to find a clue in the middle of an infinite number? We'd be better off trying to find that grain of sand."

"And to make matters worse, we don't even know what it is we're looking for," I added.

Silence descended on the room. It looked like all we had done was prove that the clue was impossible to find. Stephanie, Justin, and I stared glumly at the whiteboard with dejected looks on our faces.

Catherine, on the other hand, was staring at the bank robber's poem. She was still looking at it when she broke out into a large smile.

"I think he told us just what we are looking for," Catherine said. "In fact, he hid it in plain sight."

She read the last line of the poem out loud.

Is anybody smart enough to call upon my friend?

As Catherine read the poem, she put emphasis on the word *call*, which was all I needed to see what she was saying.

"Ten digits. Call my friend. It's a phone number!" I said. "We're looking for a phone number hidden in the digits of pi!"

"And I think the other numbers tell us where to look," said Catherine.

CHAPTER 11

Old Mike was still not back at school. Instead, we were subjected to closer and closer scrutiny by Mr. Swenson. He was following us so closely that we hadn't had a chance to leave another note in Phil's locker. From the moment we walked into the school until we left at the end of the day, it seemed that everywhere we went, he was right behind us. And it wasn't just Justin and me, either. Stephanie and Catherine said he seemed to be following them, too.

"That guy creeps me out," Stephanie complained as we walked home from school one day.

"Me, too," agreed Catherine. "Every time I turn around, he's right behind me."

"You don't even have to turn around to know he's there." Stephanie laughed. "Because that guy stinks!"

Catherine joined in the laughter as we continued to walk.

"Seriously, though, how are we going to get rid of him and get Old Mike back?" Catherine asked.

"We need to get another note into Phil's locker," I said.

"But how can we when Mr. Swenson is always watching us?" Catherine asked.

"Well, he can't follow all of us at the same time, can he?" I asked, adding, "We already proved that with the first note".

"We just need to come up with some way to distract him," Stephanie said thoughtfully.

As it turned out, Phil and Robbie Colson provided all the distraction we needed.

We hadn't heard much from the bullies in our classroom for a while. I think Agent Carlson had scared them enough that they were afraid to mess with us. That didn't mean they wouldn't mess with anyone else, though. Sniffy put thumbtacks on all the seats in Mrs. Jackson's fourth-grade class, sending three girls to the nurse's office in tears. Bill Cape dumped a pitcher of water on an unsuspecting third grader in the boy's bathroom. Bryce switched the contents of Susie McDonald's and Tim Baker's backpacks during recess, giving Susie's mom yet another excuse to yell at Mrs. Gouche.

But it was Robbie who provided us the opportunity to put another note in Phil's locker. During recess, Robbie tripped Melissa Duke, Phil's first-grade sister, as she ran to the swing set. She hit the ground hard and burst into tears. Unfortunately for Robbie, Phil saw the whole thing. Robbie may have been the biggest kid in the fourth grade, but Phil was in fifth grade and not afraid of a fight.

Things escalated quickly, and soon everyone on the playground was gathered in a large circle around the two boys as they squared off against each other.

"You tripped my little sister!" Phil snarled.

"So, what if I did?" Robbie taunted. "What are you gonna do about it?"

And with that, the fight was on. Robbie was a big boy, and he wasn't used to having anyone stand up to him. Usually a menacing glance from Robbie was enough to make anyone who thought about confronting him back down. That didn't work this time. Phil was used to being in fights, so he didn't back down an inch. It was an even match: Robbie was bigger, but Phil was quicker and very scrappy. They circled around each other and threw wild punches, but none connected. Finally, Robbie got tired of messing around and charged, tackling Phil to the ground.

Phil wormed out from beneath the larger boy and held on for dear life to one of his opponent's legs while Robbie tried to club the back of Phil's head with his fists.

I heard a whistle in the distance: one of the recess aides, probably. I looked over at Justin and nodded my head toward the building. With all the commotion, we were able to get inside without anyone seeing us. We sprinted to our classroom and wrote a quick note, then ran to hallway C. Justin kept watch while I opened Phil's locker and planted the note.

The note read:

We know what you did. You are running out of time to confess.

Justin and I made it back to the main hallway just in time. The fight was broken up, recess was over, and the halls were quickly filling with students returning to class. We strolled casually back to our classroom.

"Where did you guys go?" Stephanie asked as she came up behind us.

"Oh, we were just dropping off something for a friend in hallway C," I replied.

"Great job. But you did miss a pretty good fight," she said.

"Who won?"

"Lots of grunting and rolling in the dirt, but no blood. And since they'll probably both get a week or two of detention, I'd say they both lost."

"Good," I said. "Couldn't have happened to two more deserving guys."

Another note planted. Would our *Tell-Tale Heart* plan work?

Two days later, and still nothing. I saw Phil a few times in the hallway, but he didn't let on that anything was up.

At lunch, we discussed whether it was time to raise the stakes a little.

"The notes don't seem to be working," Catherine said.

"I know. I think he's just going to keep quiet and see if he can wait us out," Stephanie complained

"Do you think we should just tell the principal?" Catherine asked

"I don't know if she'd believe us," Stephanie replied. "We really don't have any proof that he did it."

"Then we need to get him to confess," Justin said.

Justin and I continued that same conversation as we walked through the West Bridge mall after school. My mom was shocked when I had asked her if she could pick Justin and me up from school and drop us off at the mall. I always groaned whenever she made me go shopping with her. My sister, Linda, on the other hand, could live at the mall. She and her best friend, Amy, loved to get to the mall as soon as it was open and stay until the security guards made them leave. They told my mom they were shopping, but they went mostly to look at the boys.

"I'll pick you up at six at the food court," my mom had told us as we got out of the car.

"Thanks, Mrs. Waters," Justin said as we walked toward the mall.

"And don't spoil your dinner!" she called after us.

Actually, it was Justin who had wanted to go to the mall. I could tell he had something up his sleeve, but so far, he hadn't let me know what he was up to. I knew better than to ask. Justin would tell me his plan when he was good and ready, and not before. We killed some time in the bookstore, browsing through the latest books by our favorite authors, then stopped by the toy store. We played with the remote-controlled cars until the manager asked us to leave.

"You hit one customer with a car and they throw you out," Justin complained.

"You hit three customers and a baby in a stroller," I reminded him.

"Oh yeah, I forgot about the baby." He laughed.

I checked my phone. It was almost five thirty and I still didn't know why Justin had wanted to come to the mall. I was afraid we were going to run out of time without being able to grab a snack from the food court. My mom had told me not to spoil my dinner, but since when had a large cinnamon-sugar pretzel ever slowed me down?

"Let's look in here," Justin said, stopping outside the Mr. Novelty store.

He made it sound like it was a spur-of-the-moment decision, but I could tell it wasn't. This is where he had wanted to go from the very beginning. But what was he searching for in a store full of fake bugs in ice, dribble glasses, and whoopee cushions?

I didn't have to wait long. Justin went directly to the back of the store. He knew what he was looking for and exactly where to find it. Despite his short legs, I had to break into a jog to keep up with him. And there it was, in all its multi-colored, realistic glory.

"Seriously, dude, is this really why we came here?" I asked. "Fake vomit?"

"This isn't just fake vomit," Justin said seriously. "This is what's going to help us clear Old Mike's name."

He didn't say anything more, and I didn't ask. I had learned to be very patient when Justin was hatching a plan.

My mom was waiting when we walked out of the food court twenty minutes later.

I hopped in the front seat and Justin crawled into the back. My mom took one look at me and shook her head.

"I told you not to spoil your dinner," my mom said.

"What makes you think I had something to eat?" I asked.

"Oh, I don't know. Maybe that cinnamon and sugar all over your shirt," she replied.

"You are so busted," laughed Justin from the back seat.

CHAPTER 12

The pretzel hadn't spoiled my dinner. If anything, it had made me even hungrier. I plowed through two helpings of roast beef and mashed potatoes, all swimming in a lake of rich brown gravy. I even ate the broccoli—probably my least favorite vegetable. I sat back with a contented look on my face, and my mom just looked at me and shook her head when I innocently asked if there was any dessert.

Agent Carlson called that evening and I told him we were close to solving the mysterious poem.

"Are you serious?" he asked in surprise.

"Of course," I said, adding, "It really wasn't that hard."

"We had some of our best agents work on that for months," he said. "And you're telling me that the Math Kids solved it in two weeks?"

"Well, almost solved it."

"When do you think you'll be done?"

I told him to give us until the weekend.

"Okay, I'm headed to Detroit to help out with a case, so I'll check back in with you in a couple of weeks."

I was disappointed to hear he was going to be gone for so long. I was certain we were about to crack the case.

"Who was that?" my sister asked as I hung up the phone.

"It was Agent Carlson," I answered.

"That FBI guy? Why would he be calling you?"

"We're working on a case for him."

"You're working on a case for the FBI?" She snorted in disbelief.

I nodded.

"Right, and I'm a spy working for the CIA," she replied sarcastically.

"I'm serious. You see, there was this bank robber who died. But before he died, he wrote a poem that..."

But Linda didn't stick around to hear me finish my sentence. With a shake of her ponytail, she was out of the room. I could hear the TV click on in the next room.

I smiled to myself. I didn't care if she believed me or not. We would show her when the FBI captured the remaining bank robber.

I looked over the clues we had solved from the puzzle. I knew we were looking for a ten-digit phone number hidden in pi. We also had four numbers from the clues the bank robber had left in the poem. But how did the numbers 3, 1, 7, 7, 8, and 2 help us find the phone number?

I read the poem again, concentrating on the second to last line:

Now it's time to start, right where the clues do end

Start where the clues end. Could that be it? Was the poem trying to tell us that the phone number started after 317,782 digits of pi? Could it be that easy?

I decided to try out my theory. I used the internet to find a website that listed the first million digits of pi. I scrolled through page after page of numbers, row after row of digits filling the page.

3.14159265358979323846264338327950288419716939937510582097494459230781640628620899862803482534211706798214808651328230664709384460955058223172535940812848111745028410270193852110555964462294895493038196442881097566593344612847...

On and on the numbers went. And then I realized how smart the bank robber had been. He had hidden a phone number in plain sight and years later, it was still there, just waiting to be found. And now it was up to me to find it.

I knew I couldn't just count through more than three hundred thousand numbers. It would take forever and there was no way I was going to get there without losing track. There had to be a better way.

I did a web search and found a website that allowed me to search through the digits of pi. After spending a moment to wonder how people did things before the internet was invented, I searched for the 317,782nd digit, and it returned a line of digits with one number highlighted:

747377298059504902145550108969348064510974333

If we had figured out the clues correctly, the phone number should be the next ten digits: 2145550108. There were a lot of things that could have gone wrong. Maybe we didn't get the clues right. Maybe the bank robber was leading us on a wild goose chase. But, if we got it all right and I was interpreting the poem correctly, the other bank robber's phone number was (214) 555-0108.

I did another quick internet search and looked up the location for area code 214. I smiled when I saw it was Dallas, Texas. I remembered Agent Carlson had told us that the bank robbery had happened in Dallas. I was convinced we had our guy!

CHAPTER 13

The Math Kids had a quick meeting before school the next day. We had a lot to talk about. First, I told them what I had come up with for the bank robber's phone number.

"That's great news, Jordan!" Stephanie exclaimed.

"But now what do we do?" Catherine asked. "I can't believe Agent Carlson is going to be gone for two weeks and we have to just sit on this news."

"Maybe we don't have to," Justin said.

Before we could get any more information out of him, the bell rang. We hurried down the hallway to our classroom, but not before agreeing to meet again at lunchtime.

Something happened a short while later, though, that completely changed our plans.

Just after our social studies discussion on Ben Franklin, Stephanie raised her hand to be excused to the restroom. She was returning to the classroom when she heard heavy footsteps behind her. She turned and found Mr. Swenson right behind her. She jumped back in surprise.

"What are you doing out of class?" he asked angrily.

"I was going to the restroom," she said, adding, "Not that it's any of your business."

"Everything in this school is my business," he said with a sneer. "And I always know what's going on around here."

"Yeah, what do you know?" Stephanie challenged.

"I know plenty. Like I know it was you and your friends who broke that window."

"Oh yeah? Well, I'd like to see you prove it," she said defiantly.

"I'm going to prove it, all right. And when I do, I'm going to make sure you all get suspended for it! In the meantime, you and your little friends better not cross me, or someone is going to get hurt."

"Are you threatening me?"

"That's exactly what I'm doing."

With that, he turned and stomped down the hall. Stephanie stood shaking in the hallway until Mr. Swenson was out of sight.

At lunchtime, Stephanie was still seething with anger.

"He threatened me," she said. "He said someone was going to get hurt. We have to do something about that guy, and now!"

"Do you think we should tell the principal?" asked Catherine.

"Do you think she'd believe us?" I asked doubtfully.

"Jordan's right. The only way to get rid of that guy

is for Old Mike to get his job back," said Justin. "We've got to turn up the pressure on Phil to confess."

"And how do you propose we do that?" I asked.

"It's time for Operation Puking Pupil," Justin said with a smile.

Catherine and Stephanie looked at him like he had lost his mind, but I thought I had an idea of what he meant. We spent the rest of lunch and recess discussing his plan. It was a little risky, but if we were lucky, we just might be able to pull it off.

The next day, we put Operation Puking Pupil into action. It was important for one of us to distract Mr. Swenson so the rest of us could do our part without him interfering. We waited until lunch was over and most of the students were on the playground for recess. That meant the hallways were clear, but we still had to get Mr. Swenson out of the way.

"Good luck, Justin," I said as he took off for hallway A. I gave him a few minutes to get into position before I followed him. Mr. Swenson, who was sweeping in the main hallway, paused and gave me the evil eye as I walked toward him.

"Where are you going?" he demanded.

I stammered out an excuse about needing to get a note from one of the first-grade teachers. I was lucky he didn't ask me for any details, because my mind would have come up blank. As I turned the corner to hallway A, I glanced back at the janitor as casually as I could. He was putting his broom away in the supply closet. As I watched, he turned and started walking toward the far end of the building, where Catherine and Stephanie were!

"Mr. Swenson, come quick!" I yelled at the top of my lungs.

He turned back toward me.

"Whatta you want?" he hollered back.

"There's a student getting sick!"

I could hear him grumbling as he plodded down the hallway. He stopped at the supply closet and rolled out a mop bucket. He wheeled it down the main hallway toward me.

"What is wrong with kids these days?" he mumbled as he turned the corner and saw Justin at the end of the hallway, bent over double and making loud retching sounds.

As soon as the janitor passed me, I sprinted in the opposite direction. The coast was clear, but for how long?

For the next ten minutes, Catherine and Stephanie opened as many lockers as they could and took items from each, depositing them at the bottom of Phil's open locker. Backpacks, cell phones, jackets, books, and even smelly gym shoes joined the growing pile. They left a note in each locker that pointed the finger at Phil. When Phil's locker was finally full, they pushed the door firmly closed. Catherine entered Phil's combination so all someone had to do was pull on the handle to open the locker. They quickly made their way back to our classroom as the halls began to fill with students returning from recess.

In the meantime, I hid a little present for Phil in his room. I was hoping he wouldn't find it until just the right moment. As I was walking back to our classroom,

I saw the janitor holding Justin's arm and half-pulling, half-dragging him toward the principal's office. Mr. Swenson was snarling as Justin tried to keep up with the burly janitor.

I waited anxiously for Justin to return, but he was still not back when the end of recess bell sounded. Mrs. Gouche returned from lunch just as the bell sounded to resume class, but still no Justin.

It was math time and, as usual, we broke into groups. The Math Kids were all in the yellow group, which was the most advanced math group. Mrs. Gouche assigned us a tricky problem, asking us to find a way to measure exactly four gallons of water using just one three-gallon and one five-gallon bucket. It was the kind of problem that Justin would love, but he still wasn't back, and we were starting to get worried.

DO YOU WANT TO TRY TO SOLVE THIS PROBLEM ON YOUR OWN?

YOU HAVE TWO BUCKETS: ONE CAN HOLD 3 GALLONS AND ONE CAN HOLD 5 GALLONS. CAN YOU FIGURE OUT A WAY TO MEASURE EXACTLY 4 GALLONS OF WATER USING JUST THESE TWO BUCKETS?

YOU CAN SEE THE ANSWER IN THE APPENDIX.

It wasn't until halfway through our science time that Justin finally returned with a pink detention slip clasped in one hand. As he walked by my desk, I gave him a thumbs-up to let him know we had accomplished our mission. He nodded and smiled.

"How long?" I whispered.

"A week," he responded with a shrug, as if to say, "Who cares? It was worth it".

When the bell rang at the end of the day, we hurried as fast as we could to hallway C. It was time to see if Operation Puking Pupil was a success.

The hallway was a scene of complete chaos. A large group of students was crowded around Phil's locker, all of them yelling loudly.

"Where's our stuff, dude?"

"Let us see inside your locker!"

"Yeah, open it up!"

A chant started among several in the crowd, and it grew in volume as more students joined it.

"Open it up! Open it up! Open it up! Open it up!"

Phil looked scared as the crowd around him continued to grow and the chant grew louder. Several of the larger fifth graders were now closing in on him.

"Look, guys, I don't know what you're talking about," he stammered. "I didn't take any of your stuff."

One of the larger boys—I think it was Mike Dunkin, but it was hard to see through the crowd—reached around Phil and yanked the handle of his locker. The door flew open and a pile of objects cascaded onto the floor. The crowd erupted, yelling and pushing as they tried to see if any of their belongings were in the heap. Phil looked on in disbelief. He loudly proclaimed his innocence, but no one could hear him over the growing crescendo of yelling from the crowd.

Suddenly, a booming voice sounded. "Okay, break it up! Break it up!"

The crowd looked up in surprise but continued to surge toward the locker.

"I said BREAK IT UP!" the voice yelled again, and now I could see it was Mr. Ratermann, the vice-principal, who had yelled. "Everybody, back against the wall!"

The crowd went silent and slowly backed up against the wall across from the lockers. Phil was left standing alone by his locker, its contents spilling out in a pile onto the floor. I caught his attention and pointed at my jacket pocket. He got what I was trying to tell him and reached a hand into his own jacket and pulled out the note I had put there. He looked up at me in surprise, which quickly turned to anger. He reread the note and then slowly nodded his head at me.

"What is going on here?" the vice-principal asked Phil.

Justin took a breath and stepped forward. "I can explain everything, Mr. Ratermann."

Fifteen minutes later, after the crowd in the hallway had all retrieved their property from Phil's locker (except for the pair of smelly gym shoes that no one owned up to), Justin continued his explanation in Mr. Ratermann's office. Phil was also there. I kept Stephanie and Catherine out of it. There was no sense having all of us get in trouble.

"Well?" Mr. Ratermann looked at Justin over his glasses.

"It's all part of Fourth Grade Prank Day," Justin explained.

"Fourth Grade Prank Day? I've never heard of that."

"Um, yeah," I jumped in to help Justin. "It's new this year."

"And just what prank are you playing?" Mr. Ratermann asked. The tone of his voice suggested he wasn't buying any of our story.

"Well, we found a list of locker combinations and thought it would be funny if we moved a bunch of stuff into Phil's locker as a joke," Justin said.

"And where is this list now?" Mr. Ratermann asked.

"Um, we threw it away," I answered. The vice-principal looked skeptical.

"And does this have something to do with the fake vomit?" he asked Justin.

Justin nodded. "We thought that would keep the janitor busy, so we could play our trick," he said.

"I see," Mr. Ratermann said. "And you had nothing to do with any of this, Phil?"

There was a long moment of silence. This was the moment of truth. Would Phil confess? I saw him reach into his pocket and touch the note I had left him. He gave a quick sideways glance in my direction, then took a deep breath.

"No, sir," he said. "I didn't have anything to do with this."

"But—" Justin started, but I put a hand on his arm.

I looked Phil straight in the eye. He held my gaze for a few seconds, and then looked down at his feet.

"But I do have something I want to say," he said quietly.

He went on to tell vice-principal Ratermann that he had been responsible for taking Tyler's backpack and Jackie's cell phone and putting them in Old Mike's closet. As we had suspected, he had made up the story so he could use his space camp money to buy new basketball shoes.

"You know that we fired Old Mike because of what you did, don't you?" Mr. Ratermann said sternly.

"Yes, sir. I felt terrible about that. Everyone likes Old Mike, including me," he said. "He always let me stay late in the gym after school, so I could shoot baskets. I didn't want it to turn out like it did, I promise."

"First a fist fight in the playground and now this. I'd like to see you and your parents in my office first thing tomorrow morning," Mr. Ratermann said. "We need to figure out how we are going to set this right."

"Yes, sir," Phil said as he stood up. As he walked out

of the office, my note dropped from his jacket pocket and fluttered to the carpet. Mr. Ratermann picked it up and scanned it. He turned to Justin and me and read it out loud.

"'Phil—it's your choice. Explain to the principal what you did to Old Mike or explain to the fifth-grade class why you have their stuff in your locker.' Fourth Grade Prank Day, huh?" he asked with a trace of a smile on his face. "Is it possible this was maybe done to help out Old Mike?"

"It depends," Justin said.

"Depends on what?"

"Which version gets us in the least amount of trouble," Justin said slyly.

Mr. Ratermann couldn't keep a straight face after that comment. "I think maybe I made a small mistake on your detention slip," he said to Justin. "Let me see it."

Justin smiled and pulled the crumpled pink sheet from his pocket and put it into Mr. Ratermann's outstretched hand. The vice-principal made a few marks on the paper with his pen and handed it back to Justin.

"I'm *still* getting detention?" Justin asked incredulously.

"Just one day," the vice-principal answered. "Maybe next time try coming to me first before hatching up some crazy scheme to get someone to confess."

"It might have been crazy, but it worked," I pointed out.

"True enough," he agreed. "Now, one more thing.

I'm guessing that you didn't really find a list of locker combinations. So do you want to tell me how you really got into all those lockers?"

Justin and I looked at each other. "Math," I answered.

"Math, huh?" he repeated. I expected him to ask for more information, but he let it go at that. As we got up to leave his office, he called Justin back. Mr. Ratermann reached into his drawer and pulled out a paper bag.

"Here, I believe this is yours," he said.

Justin looked inside the bag and saw the fake vomit he had purchased at the novelty store.

"You never know when you're going to need it," the vice-principal said with a smile.

"Yes, sir," Justin said.

We were almost to the door when Mr. Ratermann stopped us again.

"You know that Old Mike is lucky to have people like you looking out for him, don't you?"

We nodded.

"That's what friends do for each other, Mr. Ratermann," Justin said.

CHAPTER 14

With Old Mike's fate now in the hands of the vice-principal, we turned our attention to finding the remaining bank robber. Agent Carlson wasn't due back in town for almost two weeks and we were itching to do something now.

"What if we just call the number?" Stephanie suggested.

"But what would we say when someone answers?" Catherine asked. "Excuse me, did you happen to rob a bank fifteen years ago? Would you mind turning yourself in?"

"Well, we can't just hop on a plane and walk around Dallas looking for people who might be a bank robber," Stephanie said.

"We don't need to," I said. "I did a search of the number on Facebook."

"But you're not old enough to have a Facebook account," Stephanie said.

"No, but my sister is," I responded with a smile. "And she uses *HelloKitty1234* for all of her passwords."

We all laughed.

I pulled a crumpled piece of paper out of my pocket. "Our bank robber's name is Jeffrey Cargill and he lives at 513 Utz Lane in Fairfax, Virginia."

"Wait a minute, the bank robbery was in Dallas," Stephanie said. "If he moved to Fairfax, wouldn't he have a different area code now?"

"Not if it was a cell phone and he kept his number when he moved," I said.

"So, he lives in Fairfax. What are we supposed to do about it?" Catherine asked.

"Fairfax is only twenty miles from here," I said.

Justin clicked on his phone for a minute and looked up with a smile. "That's only ten stops away on the Silver Line train."

"Are you talking about finding the bank robber ourselves?" Catherine gasped.

"That's exactly what I'm talking about," Justin said with a sly grin. "Who wants to take a little train ride on Saturday morning?"

"Let's do it!" Catherine yelled.

And with that, we were all in.

Saturday morning was bright and sunny. It was warm, I was with my best friends, and we were on a daring quest to hunt down a bank robber. It didn't get any better than that.

We were all excited as we boarded the Silver Line train. We would be in big trouble if our parents knew what we were up to, but that only added to the excitement. We talked nonstop for the entire forty-five-minute ride to the Millwood Station. It wasn't until we had piled off the train that we began to get a little nervous. I mean, this was a guy who had committed armed robbery. What were we thinking?

"It's not a big deal," Justin assured us. "All we're going to do is walk by his house to see where he lives. It's not like we're going to try to arrest him or anything."

"I guess you're right," Catherine agreed. "But it's still a little scary, don't you think?"

"I'm not scared," I said, trying to sound brave but failing miserably.

Three blocks down Millwood Street, we saw the street sign for Utz Lane, and what we were doing suddenly became very real.

"So, are we ready for this?" Stephanie asked.

"As ready as we're going to get, I guess," I responded with just a little quaver in my voice.

Utz Lane was a quiet street of about twenty houses. They were well-kept, with neatly trimmed lawns shaded by large oak and elm trees: the leaves just filling in as the weather grew warmer. The houses were not much bigger than the ones we lived in ourselves. They were not what we had imagined for the home of a bank robber who had made off with more than a million dollars.

"With all that money, I was expecting him to own a mansion," I said. "These are just regular old houses."

"Maybe he blew all his money on fancy sports cars," Justin responded.

But the vehicle in the driveway of 513 Utz Lane was an old minivan that was dented in several places and had a large patch of rust on one of the sliding doors.

The bigger surprise was what we saw in the front yard. Twin girls, who looked to be around six, were sitting in lawn chairs next to a card table with a sign that read Lemon-Aid 50 Cents. A chipped glass pitcher of lemonade sat on the table next to a stack of plastic cups.

"Would you like to buy some lemonade?" asked the twin on the left.

"It's only fifty cents a glass," added the twin on the right.

"Is this 513 Utz Lane?" I asked.

"Yes, but my little brother calls it Butts Lane," giggled the left twin.

"He's only five and can't say a lot of words right," explained the right twin.

"He's adopted. He has special needs," said the left twin in a loud whisper.

"We're not supposed to say that," replied the other twin, giving her sister a disapproving look.

"Well, it's true, isn't it?"

"Yeah, but we're not supposed to say that."

We looked back and forth as the two girls talked. It was like watching someone talk to herself in front of a mirror.

"So, do you want to buy some lemonade?" repeated the left twin.

"Sure," I said, digging into my pocket for the dollar I had stuffed there this morning.

The twins made quick work of pouring me a glass of lemonade and carefully counted out five dimes in change. I took a small sip. The lemonade was lukewarm and tasteless.

"Do you like it?" asked the twin on the right anxiously. "We weren't sure how much lemonade mix to put in."

"Sure, it's great," I lied, not wanting to hurt their feelings.

"I can go inside and get an ice cube if it's not cold enough."

"No, it's fine, really."

"Did your dad help you make the lemonade?" Catherine asked.

"No, he's at work," replied both twins at once.

"He's a therapist at the army hospital," left twin explained.

"Yeah, he helps people with only one leg learn to walk again," right twin added.

"They've got two legs, just one of them is made of metal," left twin clarified.

"Well, they only got one real leg," right twin argued.

While the girls went back and forth, I took the time to look at the rusting minivan and the modest home in front of me. It wasn't at all what I was expecting, and I wasn't quite sure what to think.

"Hey, guys, we should get going," Justin said.

"Yeah, you're probably right," I agreed. I turned to leave, then reached in my pocket and pulled out the five dimes the girls had given me in change. I put them on the card table.

"You want another glass?" the left twin asked excitedly.

"Sure," I said.

One twin held the cup while the other carefully poured in the lemonade. I took the cup and we turned to leave.

"Thanks," I called back.

"No, thank you," said one of the twins. "Bye!"

We walked down the street in silence. When we turned the corner onto Millwood, and I was sure I was out of sight of the girls, I dumped the glass of lemonade onto the grass next to the sidewalk.

Trying to break the somber mood, I exclaimed, "Wow, that was the worst lemonade I've ever tasted."

There was no response from any of my friends as we continued walking. The silence continued until we reached the train station.

"What are we going to do?" Stephanie asked.

"What do you mean?" Catherine asked, but I was pretty sure she knew what Stephanie meant.

"We can't turn him in, can we? I mean, he's got kids, and one of them has special needs," Stephanie said.

"And he works with wounded veterans," I added. "I mean, he sounds like a pretty nice guy."

"But he also robbed a bank with a shotgun and clubbed a guy over the head," Justin pointed out.

He had a point, of course. The guy was a criminal. But it also looked like maybe he had turned his life around. And who was going to take care of his kids if he went to prison?

We sat in silence, all of us deep in our own thoughts, until the train arrived. On the trip back, the four of us stared out the window as the landscape flew by. Throughout the long ride, the clickety-clack of the train wheels seemed to be asking

what should we do?
what should we do?
what should we do?

But none of us had the answer.

CHAPTER 15

Once again, we found ourselves walking down the long quiet corridor in the FBI field office. Agent Carlson held the door open for us as we entered the Cold Cases room. There was another agent in the room, but he had his back turned to us, so I couldn't tell if it was Agent Perkins or Agent Wilson. Other than that, it was just Agent Carlson and us.

"So, what did you find?" he asked. "When I talked to Jordan a couple of weeks ago, he said you were getting close to a solution."

"We figured out the poem," I said. "You were right. Our math definitely helped out."

"And?" the FBI agent prompted.

"Well, we found a phone number for the other bank robber," Justin said. I went on to explain how we had solved the puzzle contained in the poem. Once again, it had been a team effort, with everyone contributing to the solution.

"You don't sound very excited about figuring it out,"

the agent said. "You understand that your work could put a dangerous criminal behind bars, don't you?"

"That's just it, Mr. Carlson," Stephanie started. "We're not sure that he is really a dangerous criminal."

"But how can you know that just from his phone number?" he asked, looking at each of us closely. He saw something in our faces, because his own face became very serious. "What aren't you telling me?"

"Well, when we found out he lived in Fairfax..." Stephanie started.

"You didn't go try to find him yourselves, did you?" Agent Carlson interrupted.

No one said anything at first, but I'm sure our faces gave us away. Finally, Catherine broke the silence.

"We were just going to go by to see what his house looked like," she said. "But then we met his kids."

"Wait! Are you telling me you went to his house? Do you know how dangerous that was?" he asked angrily. "This man robbed a bank at gunpoint. He knocked a security guard unconscious with a shotgun. He and his partner stole more than two million dollars. And you kids decided it was a good idea to just stroll by his house?"

"It was my idea," Justin said, his head down.

"But we all went along with it," I said in Justin's defense.

"We were just trying to help," Stephanie said.

"Help? What if one of you had been hurt? How do you think I would have explained that to your parents?"

None of us had a good answer to that question. The agent was right. We had acted on the spur of the

moment without thinking of the possible consequences. Now he was probably going to kick us out of the FBI and, even worse, tell our parents what we had done. We'd be grounded until we went to college. This could even mean the end of the Math Kids club.

The agent looked at us with our heads down and decided we had learned our lesson. "Look, I appreciate you trying to help," he said. "But in the future, how about you guys stick to the math and let the agents handle apprehending the suspects. Deal?"

"Deal," we all agreed.

"So, what makes you think this bank robber isn't such a bad guy after all?" he asked.

We went on to explain our visit to Utz Lane, meeting Cargill's twin daughters, learning he had adopted a son with special needs, and how he worked with wounded veterans. I even told him about how terrible the lemonade was. Agent Carlson took notes on everything (except my critique on the lemonade), nodding his head as we explained what we had learned. When we finished, he closed his notebook and looked at each of us in turn.

"First of all, this was great detective work," he said. "We had teams of really smart agents trying to figure out the meaning of that poem, and we got nowhere. Second, while I applaud your bravery, I don't want to hear of any of you going to a suspect's house ever, ever again. Third, I understand why you are so reluctant to put this guy in jail."

We all breathed a sigh of relief. Mr. Cargill wasn't going to go to jail. His kids weren't going to lose their father. But Agent Carlson's next words dashed all our hope.

"But," he said, "this man committed a serious crime. I am a sworn officer of the law and it is my duty to bring him to trial and do everything I can to convict him."

Our faces fell. I could see tears forming in Catherine's eyes and I blinked rapidly to fight back my own.

"I'm sorry, kids. It's what I have to do."

CHAPTER 16

The next few weeks dragged by. All our hard work seemed to have been for nothing. Even though Phil had confessed, Mr. Swenson was still patrolling the halls of the school. And although we hadn't heard anything from Agent Carlson, we knew his team of FBI agents were probably in the process of arresting Mr. Cargill, which would mean he would be taken away from his kids.

On the Wednesday before Easter, Mrs. Gouche made an announcement that would change everything.

"Class, we have a special guest this afternoon," she said. The classroom door opened, and in walked a man in a camouflaged army uniform. He leaned heavily on a metal cane as he limped across the room to stand by the teacher's desk. The class looked on in interest. Mrs. Gouche hadn't said anything about a guest, so this was a surprise to all of us. This was already better than most of her surprises, which usually turned out to be pop quizzes or extra homework.

"This is Sergeant Matthew Roberts," she announced. "Sergeant Roberts was severely injured when his vehicle was hit by enemy fire in Afghanistan. Today, he is going to tell you his remarkable story."

Mrs. Gouche pulled a tall stool from the corner and the man sat down. He took a couple of deep breaths before addressing the class.

"Thank you, Mrs. Gouche," the sergeant began. He went on to detail what had happened on that fateful day when his Humvee had been hit by a rocket-propelled grenade. He had woken up in an army hospital missing his right leg below the knee. The class was hanging on every word he said, totally wrapped up in his story.

"This wasn't what I was expecting that day." He lifted his pant leg to show a metal prosthetic leg. He knocked his cane against the leg, the loud metal clang eliciting giggles from the kids in the classroom, quickly stifled after a look from our teacher.

"It's okay to laugh," he said with a smile. "And in case you're going to ask, yes, I do set off the metal detector at the airport."

That brought a smile of relief from Mrs. Gouche.

The soldier took another deep breath. "I guess you're wondering where the remarkable part of the story is," the sergeant continued. "You see, lots of people in the military get injured. Some even die. That's part of the job, unfortunately. But the story doesn't end there."

He looked in anticipation toward the door. A slight man in jeans and an oversized sweatshirt entered.

"This is Jeffrey Cargill," the sergeant said. "And he is the remarkable part of the story."

All the Math Kids gasped. How was this possible? How did a bank robber turned physical therapist happen to make it into our classroom?

"On the day the grenade hit our vehicle, I lost more than my leg," Roberts said. "I also lost all hope. I thought I would be stuck in a wheelchair for the rest of my life. And that's when Jeff came into my life."

"Hey, I was just doing my job," Cargill said with humility.

"Well, you can say that all you want," Roberts said, putting an arm around Cargill's shoulders and giving him a quick squeeze, "but you saved my life."

Sergeant Roberts continued to explain how Mr. Cargill had worked with him, getting him fitted for a prosthetic leg, then pushing him gently into physical therapy, then pushing him harder and harder until he was walking and even jogging on his own.

"I've still got a long way to go," he said, "but I know Jeff is going to get me there."

"I don't know," Jeff replied with a smile. "You were pretty lazy at our last workout."

"You see, kids, this is what I've got to put up with," Roberts replied with his own wide grin as he aimed a playful punch at Jeff's shoulder.

The class applauded enthusiastically when Sergeant Roberts finished his talk. The Math Kids were still trying to figure out how Jeffrey Cargill had just happened to make it into their classroom, when Mrs. Gouche revealed her second surprise of the afternoon. She looked toward the doorway again, and in walked Agent Carlson, pushing a cart filled with chocolate pies.

"Because you were all so courteous to our guests this afternoon," Mrs. Gouche said, "we thought a slice of pie would be a nice afternoon snack."

"And there's no better dessert than pie, don't you think?" Agent Carlson said with a wink in our direction.

Justin, Stephanie, Catherine, and I grinned ear to ear at his double meaning of "pie."

We had hardly caught our breath from the surprise of seeing Agent Carlson when we had to gasp again. Walking in the door behind the FBI agent was Old Mike.

"And you can't have chocolate pie all by itself," Old Mike said as he revealed two large cans of whipped topping. The class cheered when they saw the janitor.

"Well, who's going to help me eat all of this pie?" Sergeant Roberts asked.

While the class clambered to the front to get a slice of pie covered in whipped cream, Agent Carlson pulled the Math Kids off to one side of the room.

"It turns out you kids were right," he said. "Mr. Cargill *is* a good guy. He turned over a new leaf after the robbery. He used some of the money from the bank robbery to go to college and study physical therapy. Over the years, he donated the rest to various charities."

"But what about your sworn duty to convict him?" Justin asked.

"Without any evidence, it would have been impossible," explained the agent. "However, Mr. Cargill agreed to confess."

"So, he *is* going to jail?" Catherine asked.

"No. I worked out a deal with the prosecuting attorney and the judge," he replied. "Mr. Cargill has agreed to perform community service instead. He'll be speaking at schools around the area about how people with disabilities are just like other people. Today was his first talk, but there'll be lots more to come."

"And he gets to stay with his kids?" I asked.

"Of course I do," said Mr. Cargill as he joined the conversation. "And that means I can teach them how to make lemonade the right way. I still can't believe you drank two glasses of that horrible stuff."

We all laughed.

"On a serious note, I really want to thank you kids for doing what you did," he said. "You've allowed me to get this big weight off my shoulders. I've been carrying it around for way too long. I think that's why Walter gave the FBI that poem. He wanted me to be free."

"I want to thank you, too," said Old Mike as he

joined our growing crowd. "But I don't think there's any way I can ever repay you for what you did for me."

"Sure you can, Old Mike," Justin said. "You can put an extra squeeze of that whipped cream onto my pie!"

Old Mike laughed and said, "You won't even be able to see the pie when I'm done with it!"

We were all still laughing and stuffing our faces with pie when I realized all our hard work had paid off after all. Our math skills had put to rest a fifteen-year-old bank robbery and helped Old Mike get his job back.

There was just one thing missing.

"Oh, and I forgot...one other thing," said Agent Carlson, reaching into a large paper sack.

No, Justin didn't get the badge he was hoping for, but even he had to admit that we all looked pretty cool in our new FBI hats.

THE END

COMING IN 2020! AN ENCRYPTED CLUE, BOOK 4 IN THE MATH KIDS SERIES. DON'T MISS IT!

WHEN STEPHANIE LEWIS FINDS SECRET WRITING IN THE MARGIN OF AN OLD BOOK IN THE LIBRARY, THE MATH KIDS HAVE A NEW PUZZLE TO SOLVE. BUT RST, THEY'LL HAVE TO LEARN ABOUT CODES AND CIPHERS AND HOW THEY CAN USE THEIR MATH SKILLS TO SOLVE THEM.

AS ONE CLUE LEADS TO ANOTHER, THE KIDS ARE DRAWN INTO THE MYSTERIOUS OLD HOUSE THAT OVERLOOKS THE TOWN. IS IT REALLY HAUNTED LIKE SOME OF THE TOWNSPEOPLE SAY? AND WHO IS THE MAN IN THE LONG BEARD WHO KEEPS SHOWING UP EVERYWHERE THEY GO?

JORDAN, STEPHANIE, JUSTIN, AND CATHERINE WILL NEED TO USE ALL THEIR PROBLEM-SOLVING SKILLS TO GURE OUT THE CLUES BEFORE IT'S TOO LATE.

APPENDIX

MELTING AN ICE CUBE

Justin's science fair project was called How the Shape of an Ice Cube Affects How Fast it Melts

You can do this experiment yourself. First, it helps to know that an ice cube melts because it absorbs heat from the surrounding air. The outer surface of the ice cube absorbs the heat and starts to melt first. The amount of heat absorbed depends on the surface area exposed to the air.

What is surface area? It's just the total area of all the surfaces. For something simple like a cube, it's just adding up the area of each of the six sides.

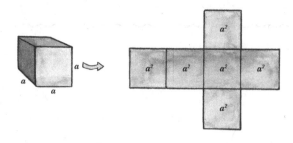

Other shapes have different formulas for calculating the surface area.

Your experiment could freeze the same amount of water into different shapes and see which ones melt faster than others. Do the shapes with more surface area melt faster or slower?

THE SEVEN WONDERS OF THE ANCIENT WORLD

The Seven Wonders of the Ancient World would be magnificent today, but were truly amazing because they were built so many years ago without the benefit of any of the modern tools we have now.

The Colossus of Rhodes was a statue of the Greek sun-god Helios. It was erected in 280 BC and stood 108 feet tall. That's about as tall as the Statue of Liberty from her feet to her crown. It was the tallest statue of the ancient world.

The Great Pyramid of Giza is the oldest and largest of the three pyramids at Giza. It was built in 2560 BC (almost 4,600 years ago). With its height of 481 feet, it was the tallest man-made structure for more than 3,800 years. It is the only one of the Seven Wonders of the Ancient World that still stands today.

The Hanging Gardens of Babylon were a series of tiered gardens said to have been built in the ancient city of Babylon. It is the only one of the Seven Wonders of the Ancient World whose location is not definitively known, leading some scholars to believe this wonder might not have been real.

The Lighthouse of Alexandria was 330 feet tall and was built during the reign of Ptolemy II Philadelphus

(280–247 BC). It was built across from Alexandria to protect ships coming into the city.

The Mausoleum at Halicarnassus is sometimes called the Tomb of Mausolus. It was 148 feet tall and was completed in 350 BC as the tomb for Mausolus and his wife. The word *mausoleum* is now used to mean an above-ground tomb.

The Statue of Zeus at Olympia was built in 435 BC. It was a 43-foot-tall seated statue of Zeus, erected in the Temple of Zeus.

The Temple of Artemis was rebuilt three times, each time bigger and grander than the last. The final temple was 450 feet long, 225 feet wide, and 60 feet tall, and had more than 127 columns.

THE MYSTERIOUS NUMBER PI

π is one of the most-talked-about numbers in mathematics. It plays an important role in anything having to do with circles. For example, to find the circumference of a circle (the distance around the circle), you can use the formula

Where
C is the circumference of the circle
r is the radius of the circle (distance from the middle of the circle to the outside of the circle)

To figure out the area of a circle, you can use the formula

Where

A is the area of the circle

r is the radius of the circle

Like the Math Kids learned, has an infinite number of digits (they never end) and there is no pattern to the digits. Because the digits don't end, you can find all kinds of numbers inside the digits of

When I was writing this book, I needed to find a phone number hidden inside the digits of π. You may have noticed in movies and TV shows that whenever they say a phone number, it always starts with 555. The phone company has reserved the phone numbers from 555-0100 to 555-0199. Nobody has these numbers, so actors can say them on TV and no one will be able to call those numbers and bother a real person. I used a website and searched for the numbers 55501 in the digits of . I found them at the 317,785th position of Since I needed three digits for the area code, I looked at the 317,782nd position and found the phone number I used in the book.

BUFFON'S NEEDLE

Can you use toothpicks to calculate the value of ? Yes, you can! More than 200 years ago, a French philosopher (and pretty good mathematician) named Georges-Louis Leclerc, Comte de Buffon figured out that you could get an approximate value for by dropping needles onto a grid of parallel lines.

Do you want to try it? Here's all you need to do:

Buy a box of round toothpicks.

Measure the length of one of the toothpicks.

On a large sheet of paper, draw parallel lines. The lines should be spaced farther apart than the length of the toothpicks.

Drop the toothpicks one at a time onto the paper.

Count the number of toothpicks that cross one of the lines.

Use this formula to estimate :

Where
L is the length of the toothpick
n is the number of toothpicks you dropped
x is the distance between the lines
c is the number of toothpicks crossing a line

For example, let's say your toothpick is 2.5 inches long and the lines are 4 inches apart. If you drop 100 toothpicks, and 38 of them cross a line, you would estimate like this:

$= 3.28947$

This result is 96 percent accurate. Not too bad for just using toothpicks! If you throw even more, you will probably get closer and closer to the actual value of , which is 3.14159 (to five digits of accuracy).

MEASURE 4 GALLONS WITH A 3-GALLON BUCKET AND A 5-GALLON BUCKET

The Math Kids were given a puzzle to measure exactly four gallons of water using just a three-gallon bucket and a five-gallon bucket. Can you do it? Give it a try before looking at a couple of solutions below.

Hint: The trick is to pour water from one bucket

into the other to get numbers other than 3 and 5. It might help to draw a picture of the two buckets and how much water they hold after each step.

Solution 1:
Fill the three-gallon bucket.
(Five-gallon bucket is empty. Three-gallon bucket holds three gallons.)
Pour the water from the three-gallon bucket into the five-gallon bucket.
(Five-gallon bucket now holds three gallons. Three-gallon bucket is empty.)
Fill the three-gallon bucket.
(Five-gallon bucket holds three gallons. Three-gallon bucket holds three gallons.)
Pour water from the three-gallon bucket into the five-gallon bucket until the five-gallon bucket is full.
(Five-gallon bucket holds five gallons. Three-gallon bucket holds one gallon.)
Empty the five-gallon bucket.
(Five-gallon bucket is empty. Three-gallon bucket holds one gallon.)
Pour the remaining one gallon of water from the three-gallon bucket into the five-gallon bucket.

(Five-gallon bucket holds one gallon. Three-gallon bucket is empty.)

Fill the three-gallon bucket.

(Five-gallon bucket holds one gallon. Three-gallon bucket holds three gallons.)

Pour all the water from the three-gallon bucket into the five-gallon bucket.

(Five-gallon bucket holds four gallons. Three-gallon bucket is empty.)

We've done it! The five-gallon bucket has exactly four gallons of water.

Solution 2:

Fill the five-gallon bucket.

(Five-gallon bucket holds five gallons. Three-gallon bucket is empty.)

Pour the water from the five-gallon bucket into the three-gallon bucket until it is full.

(Five-gallon bucket now holds two gallons. Three-gallon bucket holds three gallons.)

Empty the three-gallon bucket.

(Five-gallon bucket holds two gallons. Three-gallon bucket is empty.)

Pour the five-gallon bucket into the three-gallon bucket.

(Five-gallon bucket is empty. Three-gallon bucket holds two gallons.)

Fill the five-gallon bucket.

(Five-gallon bucket holds five gallons. Three-gallon bucket holds two gallons.)

Pour the five-gallon bucket into the three-gallon bucket until it is full.

(Five-gallon bucket holds four gallons. Three-gallon bucket holds three gallons.)

We've done it! The five-gallon bucket has exactly four gallons of water.

Note that we found two different ways to solve the same problem. There may be others, too. Lots of math problems have more than one way to solve them, so if you get stuck on a problem, it's a good idea to try a different way to solve it.

ACKNOWLEDGMENTS

I've been coaching elementary school math teams and running math camps for more years than I can remember, and I've enjoyed every minute. Coaching as many as 75 kids at one time is a challenge, but the payback is well worth it. It's a real joy to see that aha moment when a student grasps a difficult math concept.

Thanks to everyone at Common Deer Press, especially Kirsten Marion, who keeps my plots in line, and Heather Kohlmann, who does the same with my grammar and punctuation. I can't tell you how much I appreciate what you do!

One of the highlights of writing these books is to see how Shannon O'Toole will illustrate them. I love how she brings my words to life. Her pictures are truly worth more than a thousand of my words.

I had all three of my kids (and my son-in-law) at home over the holidays this year and I couldn't have asked for a better present—although the book my daughter made for me was absolutely amazing!

I was going to thank my wife for giving me the space and time to indulge in my writing career until I found out she likes the peace and quiet it provides her—so I guess it's a win-win for us.

Finally, thanks to the kids (and adults) who have read my books and contacted me with their thoughts. You can contact me at dcole.mk@gmail.com or via the Math Kids web site at http://www.theMathKids.com. I love hearing from you!

ABOUT THE AUTHOR

David Cole David Cole has always been passionate about math. His background is in math, mechanical engineering, and computer science, and he has done everything from designing missile guidance systems to teaching college computer science classes to designing data center management software.

He has coached many different math teams and ran a summer math camp for elementary school students for a number of years. He found that one of the best ways to teach math was to do it through games and stories. Most of our campers were reluctant to give up a week of their summer on math, but after attending once, they kept coming back year after year. The Math Kids series was born from the stories David told to get kids to understand and to actually like math.

David is the author of two previous books in the Math Kids series and is currently working on the next one. Check out the Math Kids website (www.theMathKids. com) to keep up with the adventures of Stephanie,

Justin, Jordan, and Catherine as they use their math skills to solve mysteries, deal with classroom bullies, and help their friends.